Who's Reading
Darci's Diary?

Who's Reading Darci's Diary?

Martha Tolles

AN
APPLE®
PAPERBACK

SCHOLASTIC INC.
New York Toronto London Auckland Sydney

ISBN 0-590-41224-8

12 11 10 9 8 7 6 5 4 3 2 1   7 8 9/8 0/9

Printed in the U.S.A.   11

to the world's best husband, Roy

Contents

That New Boy

Darci wrote in her diary, "The new boy, Travis, is really adorable!" Then she jumped up from her bed and hid her diary in her bureau drawer. Her friends were coming over in a few minutes, and she wouldn't want even them to read it. Although of course they all knew about Travis, and they had a big plan for this afternoon.

Darci ran downstairs and out the front door. She looked up and down the quiet street. No sign of her friends yet. But wait a minute, someone was out there after all—that big pest who lived across the street, Matt McGrath. He was throwing a baseball up in the air.

Matt called out between throws, "What's going on over there?" He looked at her curiously.

"Oh, nothing," she said. Actually, something was. But

1

she wasn't about to tell him about it. Only her friends knew.

If her brothers would just stay gone for a while this afternoon, she and her friends could have the house to themselves—and, most of all, the phone! Luckily, Mom was away too, at another one of those psychology classes. If Mom were here, she probably would make them go outside and play or something boring like that.

Darci stared up and down the street a moment longer. Rancho Street was short and wide and lined with small magnolia trees. The houses were California style, one- and two-story stucco, some with red-tiled roofs. It was a nice street, but Darci wished she lived closer to her friends.

Suddenly, Darci heard the phone ringing, and she raced back toward the house. It couldn't be her friends saying they weren't coming, could it? Please no, not when they had such good plans for today. She ran in the front door and reached for the phone. A girl's voice said, "Is Rick there?"

Darci told her no, that her brother would be home later. That lucky Rick! Girls were always calling him lately.

After Darci hung up, she took off her jacket and stood there for a moment, staring into the hall mirror. She fluffed back her brown hair and rolled her brown eyes. "See," she told herself, "girls call guys all the time. It's no big deal." But if it wasn't, how come her stomach—or was it her heart—was going *thump thump* now that she was thinking about doing it?

Just then the doorbell rang. Darci hurried to the front door and pulled it open. "Hi!" There were Luanne and Jill and Lee. "Hi, hi, hi!" they all said.

"C'mon in!" Darci was so glad to see her friends. "The phone's all ours."

2

"Oh, good!" Luanne beamed and held out her arm. "Look! I've got the telephone number written right here on my arm in ink." Luanne's voice was high, and it carried. Darci glanced nervously out toward the street, where Matt was now standing. He was still tossing the baseball up in the air, but he was watching them too.

"Sh-h-h-h, not so loud!" Darci pulled Luanne into the front hall, and the others crowded in behind her. Darci closed the door after them. "Let's go upstairs. Then we can do our—our thing."

"Oh, but wait a minute," Luanne said, "you haven't heard the news yet."

"Oh, yeah, tell her the bad news," Jill said.

"Wh-what?" Darci asked. How could there be any bad news when they were about to make a phone call to the adorable Travis?

"It's bad, all right," Lee said.

"You know that girl, Susan? She just moved here the end of last year."

Darci nodded. She began to get an ominous feeling. Susan was the girl who seemed to have just about everything.

"Of course, we all know who she is. Go on."

"Well"—Luanne draped herself over the staircase railing—"she's having a Valentine party at her house, and it's boy-girl, and you know who she's inviting?"

"Oh, no!" Darcy stared at Luanne's round, usually smiling face. But she wasn't smiling now.

"She's inviting Travis."

"And—and we're not invited?"

"Of course not." Luanne shrugged. "She's only having her friends—and boys."

"It'll sure ruin Valentine's Day, won't it?" Jill ran her tongue nervously over her braces.

3

"You know it," Lee agreed.

"Well, let's go ahead with our plan anyway," Darci said. She started up the stairs, but she didn't feel so happy now either. "Anyhow," she said over her shoulder to her friends, "Valentine's Day isn't till next month. Maybe—uh —maybe Susan'll move away or something before then." It wasn't a whole lot to hope for, but anyhow they might as well go ahead with their plan for today.

At the top of the stairs, Darci headed for the phone. "So let's do it," she said. She took the phone off the hall shelf and set it down on the rug. "Now we can all get around it, really close." It was a green phone with push-button numbers on it.

They all stood looking down at it. "But who's going to actually do it?" Luanne sat down quickly by the phone.

"Not me." Jill kneeled across from her. "I'd be too scared." She sucked air loudly through her braces.

"Me either! No way!" Lee sat down cross-legged. "Darci, you know the most guys. You do it." That was true, of course, since Darci had two brothers, and several boys lived on her street.

Darci sat down on the floor too and looked around at all of them. All of a sudden, she didn't feel that good about calling Travis either. Because that's what they were going to do—call Travis, only the cutest boy in the whole sixth grade!

"Well, I don't mind calling the number and even asking if he's there—if he just isn't. But if he is—"

"Then what?" Luanne was smiling again now. She wiggled closer to the phone. "What shall we say? How 'bout, 'We wish you'd come over to see us some day!' "

They all laughed. "Oh, come on!" Jill shook her short, dark hair. "I dare you to say that."

"Wel-l-l-l." Luanne eyed the phone longingly, but still

she didn't touch it. "It's probably what Susan would say," she said wistfully.

"Let's do it together." Darci reached for the phone. She didn't want to think anymore about Susan now. "You dial and I'll talk first, and then you have to."

"Okay." Luanne began to dial, reading the numbers off her arm, although they all knew his number anyway. Darci held the receiver between them so they could both hear. But the line was busy, and every time they tried the number it was still busy.

"Well, so it's no deal!" Darci hung up. She felt sort of relieved. "Let's go into my room for a few minutes, then we'll call again." She stood up.

"It's so hard to think about anything else," Luanne groaned, getting up too. "You don't have any cookies, do you?"

"I might not be able to eat right now," Jill said. "What else can we do while we're waiting?"

"We don't have any cookies anyway," Darci said. "Mom's trying to cut down on our sugar. Come on in my room." She led them into her bedroom and snapped on her clock radio to some music. Her room had yellow curtains, a green carpet, a bookcase with horse books in it, and a bureau with a diary in it. But no way was she going to show it to them, not with all that stuff she'd written in it. Because Mom was taking a course in psychology, she'd told Darci to write down anything she felt like writing. "Just let it all hang out," she'd said. Well—Darci had!

"Did you notice what Susan was wearing today?" Jill said, flopping down on the bed.

Darci went over to her bookcase. "Do you want to look at my horse books?" She handed some around. "What was she wearing?" Jill knew everything because she sat across the aisle from Susan.

"Designer jeans!"

"Designer jeans!" the rest of them echoed.

"You must be kidding," Lee scoffed.

Darci remembered now that she'd thought blond Susan looked especially good today. Lucky Susan anyway. She had earrings, she was nine months older, and she'd probably know how to throw a great boy-girl party. She certainly knew how to boss everyone around when she was hall monitor.

"I'd give anything to go to her party," Luanne said, "even though I don't like her. I'd even give up cookies." Luanne set the horse book Darci had given her on the bedside table. No one seemed to be in the mood for horses right now.

"But you don't really know her," Lee pointed out.

"True, but how can you like somebody who has everything?" Luanne frowned.

"It makes it hard, doesn't it?" Darci had to agree. Susan didn't seem to be a bit afraid to go up to Travis and talk to him in the halls either.

"Well, I wish we could do something special for Valentine's Day." Jill frowned. "But I know my mom wouldn't let me have a boy-girl party. No way!"

"Me either," Lee said. "But it isn't fair. Susan should ask the whole class."

"If Darci had a party, she'd probably have to invite Matt McGrath," Lee giggled.

"Oh, for sure," Luanne agreed. "But I can think of worse things."

Darci shrugged. "Oh, he'd never come." Matt McGrath would never like girls. Never! "But I wish we could do something really far out for Valentine's Day," she added, "instead of just cards and cookies in the classroom." What she really wished was that her mother would let her have a boy-girl party. Lucky Susan. Her mother must be different.

"You're right," Lee was saying. "I mean, we *are* in sixth grade!"

"At least we could send Travis a valentine," Darci suggested to the others.

"Oh, fantastic!" Luanne beamed. "Let's get the biggest, most gorgeous one, all covered with lace and—"

"—and lots of hearts, and we'll write 'I love you' all over it," Jill added, sucking air madly through her braces.

Just then, Darci heard a car go by out front. "I hope that isn't Rick!" she exclaimed. Rick drove an old Honda to high school every day, and he was due home soon.

She jumped up and peered out the window, but it wasn't her brother's old Honda going down the street after all. "Listen, let's hurry up and make our call before my brothers get here. Rick'll want to use the phone, and Donny will want to listen in on us." She gathered up the rest of her horse books and dropped them on the bedside table.

"Okay," Luanne said. "I'm ready."

They all went out into the hall and huddled around the phone again, although Darci was beginning to wish now they hadn't started this whole thing. Travis would probably rather talk to someone like Susan. What would they say to him? What good would it do? Was he going to pay any attention to them? When every girl in the whole sixth grade liked him?

"Let's get it over with," Darci said. She reached for the phone, dialed, and held the receiver toward Luanne. But this time a little kid's voice answered.

"Hullo," he shouted into the phone, "who do ya want?"

Luanne held the receiver close to her mouth, but she suddenly stared up at Darci like someone in a coma.

"Who is it?" the kid's voice bellowed on the other end of the phone.

Luanne closed her eyes and dangled the receiver over to Darci. "I—I can't," she whispered.

Darci took the receiver with a sticky nervous hand and put it up to her ear, but somehow her mouth was frozen shut.

"Hey, you, I'm gonna hang up," the kid threatened now. "Say something!" Darci heard a click on the line and thought maybe he already had.

"Uh—is—uh—is" she started to say. The other girls motioned wildly to her to keep talking. "We—uh—want to —talk to your brother, Travis." Ah, she got it out at last.

"Travi-i-i-i-s!" the little kid yelled right next to the phone. "Telephone. It's a gir-r-r-l. A girl wants to talk to you, Travis."

Darci looked around at the others, awestricken. "He's there. He's coming to the phone!" She thrust the phone at Luanne, then Jill, then Lee, but they all shook their heads frantically.

"No, no. You do it," they whispered.

"Hello." They could all hear Travis's voice answering now. Travis, the biggest, the best-looking boy in the whole sixth grade. She couldn't do it! Darci quickly smashed down the receiver into the hook. She hunched over, burying her face in her hands.

"No way!" she said. "I—I'm sorry, but I couldn't." She closed her eyes for a moment. "He said 'hello,' " she said dreamily. How nice his voice had sounded over the phone. "Hello." It echoed in her ear.

"Oh, Darci, why'd you do that?" Luanne protested.

"Darci, you didn't have to get scared—just because we were," Jill added.

Suddenly, they heard voices coming from downstairs.

8

"Hey, Darci-i-i!" It was her little brother, Donny. "Where's Mom? Me and Matt are getting something to eat." Matt? Was he in the house? Darci looked at her friends, aghast.

"Mom's not here," she yelled back. Then she whispered to her friends, "Do you think they heard us?"

"Oh, yikes! I hope not," Luanne exclaimed. "They'd tell for sure."

"Let's go downstairs." Darci jumped to her feet. "I don't know why Matt's in our house anyhow. Maybe he's just trying to spy on us."

"He does seem to hang around your house a lot," Luanne said.

Darci shrugged. "I know. He's always sort of bugging me. But, well, Donny and Rick both like him. C'mon. If I can get a look at him I can tell, maybe, if he heard anything or not."

They hurried down the stairs and out to the kitchen where Matt and Donny were. Her little six-year-old brother was pouring milk into a glass. Matt glanced over at them with a knowing smile.

"Hi," he said.

Donny looked up and kept pouring. The milk flooded across the counter and down onto the floor. "Darci, guess what? I'm getting a new pet tomorrow."

"Donny, the glass is full! Stop pouring!" Darci protested. "What kind of a pet?" It couldn't be anything very exciting. Mom had said no dogs or cats because she was too busy right now with all the psychology classes.

"I'm not going to tell. It's a secret."

Darci glanced over at Matt. He was still standing there with that funny smile on his face. Why? What was so funny?

"At last you're off the phone," Donny said. "Matt's

9

been trying to use it. Go ahead, Matt." Donny got a sponge and began to mop milk all over the counter. Darci realized suddenly that Matt was standing right next to the kitchen phone.

"What's the matter with his own phone?" Luanne put in.

"It's not working," Donny said. "His mom said so. Go ahead, Matt." Donny was trying to act big just because Matt was there, Darci could tell.

"Thanks, Donny." Still, Matt smiled in that funny way as he leaned toward the phone. "So I have to call the phone company. But I wouldn't want to interrupt anybody's calls, of course," he said. And the way his blue eyes looked over at her, as if something was terribly—fantastically—funny!

Oh, no! Now Darci remembered that click on the phone before. He'd heard! He must have. She had to get out of here.

"Let's go," she said to her friends.

They backed out of the kitchen and went to the front hall, where they formed a huddle. "Did you hear what he said?" Darci whispered.

"Yes," they exclaimed. "What do you think?"

"The worst!" Darci groaned. "Just the worst! He heard —I know he did."

"Oh, no!" Luanne said. "What if—what if he tells everybody?"

"See Ya Tomorrow"

"If that Matt McGrath heard our phone call, I'll freak out!" Darci wrote in her diary that night. Darci thought her diary was the greatest. It was a brown leather book, like a small journal or notebook.

She liked to write in it about everything, let it all hang out, as Mom had suggested. She guessed Mom said such things sometimes because she wanted to sound like the teacher of her psychology class. Darci wished Mom and the psychology teacher didn't have so many strict ideas though. A diary—that was a good idea. No parties with boys—that was a bad one.

Anyway, Darci had written that Travis had dark eyes and dark curly hair, that once she'd held his hand when they had square dancing in PE, and that she'd never kissed a boy and she wondered what it would be like. It was really neat to write about her friends and the things they did, and sometimes about the things that bugged her too—like the way Susan bossed everyone around so much and talked to Travis a lot.

Tonight, Darci wrote all about the whole phone call to Travis, and whether Matt was listening in. Then she wrote about Susan's party. If only something would happen. Maybe Susan would invite them all, or maybe Susan would get a flu bug or move away and have to cancel her party. When Darci finished, she hid the diary in her second bureau drawer. NO ONE must ever get to read it! Not her friends, especially not her brothers, not even her parents. She could trust Mom not to look at it. Dad too. Besides, Dad wouldn't be interested in all that stuff about boys.

The next day at school, Darci and her friends talked about the phone call again.

"What do you think Matt would do if he heard?" Lee asked.

"He'd tell." Luanne shook her ponytail.

"That'd be so rotten." Jill sucked air through her braces.

"I wish there was some way to find out," Darci said. "We could try to tell him it was just a joke or—or—" Darci paused. What could they tell him? It was going to be so hard to pass Travis in the halls now. "And when we see Travis, we won't know—" Darci broke off. There, suddenly coming toward them, was that Susan.

"Sorry, kids," Susan said, bearing down on them. "You can't just stand around and clog up the halls." Susan was wearing a tag that said Hall Monitor, and she spoke in a loud, important-sounding voice, as if she were their mother. "Go out to the playground and keep the halls clear." She shook back her short, blond hair. She wore green earrings that just matched her green sweater.

Darci and Luanne glanced at each other. Did they have to let this girl boss them around?

"We were only talking," Darci explained. The earrings looked like jade.

"Well, you know Mrs. Blair says no standing around and yakking in the halls," Susan said. Mrs. Blair was the principal and liked the halls to be quiet.

"Okay, so we'll go," Luanne said.

They moved slowly down the hall until they reached the doorway to the playground. "Susan thinks she's so big, doesn't she?" Luanne said, glancing back over her shoulder. "No standing around and yakking," she mimicked. "And did you get a good look at those earrings?"

"I did," Darci said. "They looked like real jade, didn't they?"

"Have to keep the halls clear," they heard Susan calling out to another group of kids.

"That's the third pair of earrings I've seen her wear," Jill said enviously.

They pushed open the doors and went out into the cold air.

"Let's go get a volleyball," Darci said.

"Too late." Lee shrugged. "If you don't get there early, they're all gone. They don't have enough volleyballs."

"It seems like there oughta be enough volleyballs for the sixth graders," Luanne complained. "What's the good of being the oldest in the school, I sometimes wonder."

"I know what you mean," Darci agreed. They'd all looked forward to this year, but it didn't seem to make that much difference after all.

Darci glanced across the playground just then, and she

saw, coming toward them, Travis—Travis with another sixth-grade guy named Brian.

"Pss-s-s-t, look who's coming," she whispered. He was walking right this way. With his dark eyebrows and eyes and dark hair that fell across his forehead, he was so good-looking!

"Oh, no," Luanne moaned. "What'll we do now?"

The four of them drew closer together and tried not to look at him. But it was hard not to look at Travis. And besides, Darci had to study his face and try to figure out if he knew—about their phone call.

But now he looked over at them. Then he definitely turned to say something to the guy, Brian, with him. Then they both laughed and glanced over at the girls again. Oh no! What were they laughing at?

After they'd passed, the girls huddled together and stared at one another in horror. "Do you think he knows?" Darci exclaimed.

"I know he knows." Luanne was positive.

"What a bummer," Jill said.

"How'll we ever dare send him a valentine now?" Lee added. "What'll we do?"

Just then the bell rang, so the only thing to do at the moment was go to class.

"I know what," Darci said as they started down the hall to class. "When I get home today, I'm going to talk to that Matt McGrath! I'm just going to tell him off!"

Darci went home that afternoon steaming. She'd hang around out front, wait for Matt to show, tell him to stay out of her phone calls.

She stared up and down Rancho Street for a while. A gardener down at the end of the street pushed a power mower back and forth across a yard. Partway up the street, a Japanese magnolia tree had bloomed, and its blossoms were a burst of lavender color. It could have been a nice day, if only she weren't so worried. But there was no sign of Matt, so after a while Darci went into her house. As she was going upstairs, she heard Donny talking to someone in his room. She hurried to his doorway.

"Donny—"

"Darci, look! I've got my new pet. Isn't he neat-o?"

Donny was crouched on the floor with a metal cage in front of him. In it was a small, brownish hamster.

"So that's who you were talking to!" Darci had to laugh. She went in and knelt beside the cage. "He looks cute, Donny."

"You wanna hold him?" Donny scooped the hamster out of his cage and thrust him toward Darci.

"Well, okay." She cuddled the hamster in her hands. He was soft and warm and little. She stroked him slowly while she was thinking. "Donny, yesterday when you and Matt were in the kitchen—"

"And I'm naming him Bwana," Donny interrupted.

"Bwana?" Darci laughed again. "Bwana! But that's an African word. It means *master.*"

"Don't laugh." Donny scowled. He hated to be laughed at. "Besides, he likes the name."

"Oh, sure." Darci started to smile and then remembered not to. "Listen, Donny, I was going to ask you—"

Downstairs she heard the front door opening and now footsteps below and voices. Rick was talking to someone. They must be out in the kitchen. Now they were coming upstairs. Then she heard Matt's voice. Oh, now was her chance, but what could she say? "Did you listen in on my phone call?" If he hadn't heard anything, he and her brothers would wonder what she was so worried about. They'd guess she'd been calling a boy!

"Matt's collecting aluminum cans," Rick said from the

doorway. "What's going on in here?" Matt had a plastic sack hung over his shoulder. Darci looked hard at him, his blue eyes, the freckles on his nose, his seemingly friendly face, and tried to figure out what he knew.

"Look what I got, Rick. A new hamster!" Donny exclaimed.

"Hey, he's cool." Rick came into the room and took the hamster. They all crowded around.

Donny began to jump up and down on his bed. "And I'm going to take him to school and—" He made a tremendous leap in the air and came down with a sharp crack. The bed banged down on the floor.

"Donny!" Darci exclaimed. "You broke the leg off your bed!"

"Oh, yikes!" Donny slid off the bed and looked worried.

"Mom isn't going to go for that," Rick said.

Actually, Darci knew Mom wouldn't be that cross about it. In some ways, Mom wasn't that strict, but in others—

"Maybe you could fix it," Matt said. "Prop it up with something."

"You better tell Mom, I think." Darci left the boys down on their hands and knees, inspecting Donny's bed. No chance of talking anymore to Matt now. It wouldn't be exactly easy, anyway, to ask him.

She went downstairs to the kitchen for a snack. If he did tell—and she thought of the way Travis had laughed at them today. She frowned and plunged her hand into a box of crackers, but it was empty. She reached for some bread. Gone! The fruit bowl—nothing! Darci sighed. The boys had gotten everything.

And then the phone rang. "Hello," a voice said.

"I'll go get my brother," Darci answered, hardly listening.

"Hey, now just wait a minute. What makes you think I

want to talk to your brother anyway? Isn't this Darci?"

Darci leaned against the kitchen table. There was suddenly something about that voice! The whole room was practically reeling and swimming before her eyes. "Y-y-yes." She managed one word.

"Do you know who this is?"

What a question! She didn't know, not really. She could wish. Oh, how she could wish!

"It's Travis," the voice said.

"Oh, Oh. Uh—hi." A hot feeling burst out all over her.

"Hi. How're ya doing?"

How was she doing! Fine. Terrible. She felt like someone with the flu—hot, weak, shaky legs. She collapsed onto the kitchen chair.

"I—I'm okay."

"Well, say, could you help me?"

Help him? She'd run through the snows of Alaska for him! "Why sure," she exclaimed.

"I'm trying to find Matt McGrath," he explained. "And his mom said he might be over there at your house. I have to talk to him about the volleyball game tomorrow."

Despair, disappointment surged over her. So that's all he wanted. "He's here," she said, bleakly. "I'll go get him." He hadn't called to speak to her after all. She needn't run through the snows of Alaska, just upstairs.

"But, Darci, listen. I'll see ya tomorrow at school, okay?" he added.

So maybe he had called to speak to her, and he'd just used Matt as an excuse. Darci swept up the stairs with winged feet. "See ya tomorrow!" Travis had said that to her!

"Matt," she called. How happy her voice sounded. "Telephone for you. It's Travis."

"Me?" Matt came out into the hall. "Okay." He headed

for the phone, then glanced quickly back at her. "Did you have a great talk, Darci?" He looked so amused.

Oh, he knew, all right—about her call and how she felt about Travis. But what did she care now? She was going to talk to Travis tomorrow maybe. She hurried into her room and over to her bureau. She opened her second drawer, lifted up her clothes, and dug out her diary. She must write about this, about talking to Travis on the phone.

She sprawled on her bed and quickly scribbled in her diary. "Seeing Travis tomorrow maybe." And then she added, "I wish I could look older. Like that Susan, and have green earrings."

She squinched her eyes shut for a moment, picturing Travis. "He is adorable," she breathed softly to herself, and then she wrote that down too. She closed the diary with a snap. But right now, while the boys were busy in Donny's room, would be such a good time to use the phone. She jumped up and darted for the door. She'd run downstairs and call Luanne and Jill and Lee and tell them what Travis had said: "See ya tomorrow!"

The Missing Diary

Darci stared at herself in the mirror. She frowned at her feathery brown hair and brown eyes. She fastened a clip in her hair to hold it back. If only she had some neat gold earrings that would shine when she shook back her hair —or green jade ones. She shook back her hair. All she saw was—earlobes! Maybe she would ask Mom again—now!

She stood way back from the mirror and almost closed her eyes for a minute. Now she looked okay. At least she wasn't too anything, like too thin or too fat or too tall. Would Travis really talk to her today? What would they talk about anyway? Maybe she should ask Rick for some ideas.

Darci hurried downstairs to breakfast. Everyone was

already at the kitchen table. Dad and Mom were reading the paper. Rick and Donny were eating.

Darci sat down and began to eat her grapefruit. She could see that Mom was reading the editorial page of the *Los Angeles Times*. It wouldn't be good to interrupt Mom just when she was worrying about world problems. But Mom looked up.

"Good morning, Darci."

"Grapefruit's dangerous," Donny said, covering his face with his napkin as he dug into his. "They can get you right in the eye."

Darci ignored him. Now, while Mom was looking at her, would be a good time. "Mom, there's this girl. She's in my class. She's only a little older than I am." Oh, mistake. Why did she even mention age? "And she wears earrings to school every day. And she's having a boy-girl party."

"Hey-y-y-y." Rick reached for the sports section. "Darci's getting older," he mocked.

Dad lowered the newspaper and looked at Darci with interest. Dad had new wire-framed glasses which Darci thought were neat. She hoped he was going to say, "Why, yes, Darci is old enough for those things."

But instead he smiled a little and said, "I'd say boys are pretty nice people, but I think it's up to Mom."

"Darci." Mom leaned over and patted Darci's arm. "Listen, dear, my psychology teacher and I both think there's too much pressure put on boys and girls these days to grow up too soon. I really think we should wait a bit."

A bit, Darci wanted to say. How long was that? About five years?

Mom jumped up and hurried over to the oven. "Oh, my, the bran muffins are ready. I almost forgot them."

"I'm never going to have any boy-girl parties." Donny waved his spoon around. "Not me! No girls ever."

"Be quiet," Darci said bitterly. He was such a little kid. She should have known it would be no use to ask about a party. As for earrings, well, for now anyway, she'd just have to talk to Travis without any. She'd try to keep her hair over her ears.

"Rick, what do you talk to girls about? Like between classes, do you talk to them?" Darci began to eat her grapefruit. She noticed for the first time that Rick had a little piece of bloody tissue on his chin. He must have cut himself shaving again. He was hoping to get an electric razor soon, she knew.

"Me? Talk to girls?"

Mom set a plate of muffins on the table, and Rick reached over and took three. "Sure, I talk to them if they're lucky."

Rick thought he was quite the big shot these days since he'd started shaving once a week. Sometimes Darci felt like pointing out that Dad shaved every day, but she didn't.

"Well, I just wondered what you talk about."

"Why don't you talk about pets?" Donny slurped up his cereal. "That's what I like."

"Better do less talking"—Mom carried some dishes over to the sink—"and get moving, or you'll miss your bus. Donny, make sure that door on the hamster cage is shut tight. Darci, are you ready?"

"Almost, Mom."

Dad put down his paper. "Well, I must be off. Learn a lot today, kids." He smiled at them. That was the standard joke around home.

"I am, Dad," Donny exclaimed. "I can read a whole lot now."

For a moment, Darci was almost sorry to hear that. Could he read a diary?

Dad reached for his briefcase on the floor, then stood up. "Don't work too hard today," Mom said. "My teacher and I both think—"

"I can guess." Dad leaned down and kissed her. "I promise not to work more than twelve hours. How's that?" he kidded.

Darci glanced at the clock. It was getting late. She jumped up and headed for the stairs to go get her pack. There was no more time now. She'd have to think about what to say to Travis later.

In her room, she stopped for a second in front of the mirror. Did her blue pants and shirt look good? She pulled on a sweater and slipped her pack on her back. She leaned toward the mirror. "Hi, Travis," she breathed softly. "Do you like—uh—music?" Or should she say *pets*? Or *food*? She flattened her hair over her ears. Why did Mom have to be so strict? Why was Susan so lucky?

She heard Rick out front drive off in his Honda to high school. His friend from down the street, William, would be with him as usual. Darci ran downstairs again.

"Bye, Mom, Dad," she called. "C'mon, Donny." She and Donny hurried out the front door and up to the corner of Rancho Street and Robles Avenue to wait for the bus. Some other kids were already there. One of them was Matt McGrath. As she went toward him, she suddenly realized Matt might have actually helped her! Maybe the reason Travis was getting interested in her was because Matt had told him she'd called him. Wouldn't that be a laugh! That would be a good one on Matt! He might have done her a real favor.

"Hi, guys," she said, joining the group at the corner. Donny's friend, Jon, was there too and a couple of others.

"What's the joke, Darci?" Matt eyed her.

"Oh, nothing." Darci swished back her hair and had to look away so she could really smile. If his telling had helped, that would be so funny actually. And today she would find out!

The bus was coming down Robles Avenue now, the morning traffic swirling past. When the bus stopped, the kids swarmed up the steps and squeezed down the aisle looking for seats. There weren't very many left. Darci quickly grabbed one and pushed Donny into it and sat down next to him. As they rode along, she tried to think. What would she say to Travis? If only she could say, "Why don't you come over sometime?" And after he said yes, she'd say, "I hear Susan is having a big Valentine party." That lucky Susan would never invite Darci and her friends.

And he would say, "Yeah, but I don't know if I'll go or not."

And she would say, "I hear it's going to be really small." If only she could say, "Come to my party instead." If only Mom—

"Hey, Darci, we're here," Donny yelled in her ear.

The bus was already pulling up before the low, tan stucco building of the Rio School. And everyone was pushing and shoving to get off, and yelling and laughing. As soon as Donny jumped down the steps, he went running off to the kindergarten playground. Darci followed, looking all around for her friends. She almost bumped into Matt, who was right behind her. But there were her friends already, waiting on the sidewalk for her.

"Hi." Darci waved, hurrying toward them. She'd talked to each one on the phone last night, so they all knew she might talk to Travis today. They closed in on her in a huddle—like football players.

"Darci, listen, when do you think he'll talk to you?" Luanne's voice was so high! Darci looked around nervously. There was Matt right behind her.

"O-o-o-h," he mocked in a silly high voice and raised his eyebrows at them and grinned. He must have heard!

"Matt!" Darci exclaimed. She gave a quick frown to the others. "Stop hanging around."

She and her friends moved into a tighter huddle and went off down the hall together. "That Matt," Darci exclaimed. "He's always part of the scenery!"

"I've noticed," Luanne said.

"Darci, what're you going to do today? About Travis? What're you going to say?" Jill licked her lips excitedly.

"I don't know. I've been trying to figure it out. I just might freak out or something!" She felt safe with all her friends around her, but if she were all alone— "Listen. Let's be sure to stick together today, okay?"

"But we always do." Lee sounded hurt.

"I know, but more so. I—I don't want to meet him alone."

"You don't?" Luanne beamed. "Sure, we'll stay with you, won't we, you guys?"

All morning, Darci watched for Travis between classes, but she didn't see him, and nothing happened. She and her friends were all together again after lunch, getting a drink of water, when suddenly round the corner came Travis.

"Hi," he said.

Darci looked up from the drinking fountain, but somehow she must have leaned on the handle just then, because the water shot straight up into her mouth and her left eye. For a moment, she was blinded.

She choked on the water or the air or something and wiped her eye and mouth. "Hi," she managed to gasp.

Luanne slapped her on the back while she coughed and tried to breathe.

"Hey now." Travis grinned. "Cool it!" He leaned one elbow casually against the wall and watched her. "You can stop beating on her now," he said to Luanne. "I think she'll make it."

Darci pushed back her hair, then quickly pushed it forward again to cover her plain old ears. "Oh, sorry," she said. She knew she must be all red in the face from bending over and choking. Still, it had given her a chance to think for a minute. Quick! She must say something really fast. But what would it be? The guys on her street were always interested in food, but after that—

"Sorry it took so long to get Matt to the phone yesterday," she plunged in. "But he was upstairs looking at my brother's hamster." Those dark eyebrows and those dark eyes. How her heart quaked in her chest! How could her mouth speak those words in such a normal way?

"A hamster, huh? Those are neat little things. I used to have one of them a long time ago." His dark eyes gazed down at her. "When I was a little kid," he added.

"And guess what my brother's going to call him?" she hurried on nervously. "Bwana. That's African for *master*." Of course, Travis probably knew that already.

"Ha ha," he laughed, and so did her friends, so maybe telling the name was a good idea.

"Yeah, hamsters are okay," he added. "I used to let my hamster run in those tube things you put on top of the cage."

So pets were the way to go! Donny was right! Let's see, she could talk next about the goldfish Donny used to have. But how hot she felt with this sweater on!

"So maybe I'll come over and see him sometime."

Now she was burning up inside her clothes.

"Oh—uh—great!" she was saying, when a voice called loudly, "Hi, everybody." It was Susan—Susan with her important-sounding voice as if she were about sixteen. Now she was hurrying toward them.

"Oh, no," Jill groaned under her breath.

"Pretend you didn't hear," Luanne whispered.

Darci quickly motioned toward her friends as they all clustered around Travis and turned their backs toward Susan.

"Hi," Susan said again. This time they had to turn around to look at her. She stood there smiling at them. Darci knew she couldn't smile back. Just when she was talking to Travis, who needed Susan?

"Look, you guys, I'm sorry but you have to go outside. You know how it is." She looked at Darci and the others. "You know, I'm hall monitor." Then she turned to Travis. "But, Travis, I wanted to tell you—" Her earrings shone softly behind her hair. She lowered her voice and said something to him. She was wearing a snazzy-looking T-shirt that said Luv Ya on it. Darci wished she had a T-shirt just like that.

So Darci and Luanne and Jill and Lee had to start moving slowly down the hall. It didn't seem fair that Susan could send them outdoors while she kept Travis in with her. That Susan had all the luck. They hung around near the door to the playground, not quite going out there.

"Did you see that great outfit she was wearing?" Jill whispered.

"You have to go outside," Susan called, looking past Travis at them.

This time they obeyed her. But after they were out of the building, Luanne exploded. "Would you listen to her! You have to go outside," she mimicked. "Susan really thinks she's the big cheese, doesn't she? She just wants to be alone with Travis."

"Look how fast she got rid of us," Jill agreed. "What's so bad about a few kids standing around in the hall anyway? Just because there're a few little rules!"

"And just when Travis was saying he might come over!" Darci groaned. She felt half-sick about it. She'd never get up the nerve to talk to him again.

"But, Darci, you were really with it," Lee said. "I mean telling him about the hamster and all that."

"Yeah, you were cool," Luanne said, "after you stopped choking. Do you think he really might come?"

"I don't know." Darci frowned. Now that he was busy inside there talking with Susan, he'd probably forget all about it. "I'd be sort of scared if he did," she admitted.

"We could come over and help," Luanne said quickly.

"Oh well." Darci shrugged. "He probably won't come anyway." Now it seemed like a very tiny possibility.

Still, he had said it, and she kept thinking about it all through the rest of her classes. When she got home that afternoon, she rushed right upstairs to get her diary. She wanted to write it all down, everything he'd said, and how that bossy Susan broke it up. And she wished she had a Luv Ya T-shirt too.

At the top of the stairs, she saw a note from Mom propped by the phone. "Gone to school meeting," it said. "Back by four. Please take care of Donny when he comes home from Jon's house."

Good, Darci thought. So while everything was quiet here, she'd get all these things written down in her diary. Mom was always trying to help at school by going to those PTA meetings—hoping to get more equipment and books for the kids, and stuff like that.

She flung her books on her bed and went straight to her bureau drawer and dug in under the clothes. But where was her diary? She opened all the drawers and poked around, but still no diary. That was weird. She checked her desk, her bookcase, her bedside table, where she often left a few books stacked, and under her bed too. Nothing. She frowned, staring around her room, then went over to look through her bookcase again. Maybe her mother had stuck it in there. But no, it wasn't there. Now, that was really strange. She was usually very careful with it.

The fronds of a palm tree outside her window moved shadows across her room like long, dark, spooky fingers. Her stomach tightened with worry. What if someone found her diary—and worse yet, read it? All those things she'd said in it about Travis, like how adorable he was. She wouldn't want anyone to see them! Not anyone! But maybe her diary was downstairs, somewhere around the house. Maybe Mom would know when she got home. But right now she'd go search the whole house.

Who Took It?

Darci searched and searched for her diary. But it wasn't anywhere. Anyway, she couldn't remember ever taking it out of her room, not even once. But still, it had to be somewhere—unless someone had stolen it!

"Listen, everybody," she said to her family after dinner. They were all sitting in the den. Rick and Mom sat on the couch, and Dad in his big leather chair. Donny was down on the floor with his hamster.

"Has anybody seen a small brown book of mine, sort of like a small notebook?" She didn't call it a diary, because she didn't want them to know she'd been keeping one. "It's the one Mom gave me." She looked hard at her brothers to see if they looked guilty.

"No way-y-y." Rick stood up and stretched. "I've gotta go do my homework. I'll let you know if I see it. Tell me if my fans call me on the phone." He grinned at her as he casually strolled from the room. Rick didn't even seem interested, much less guilty.

"What's so good about an old notebook?" Donny crouched over his cage, admiring his hamster. He didn't seem to care either.

Dad looked up from the computer magazine he was reading. "A notebook, Darci? Is it pretty important?"

"It is to me, Dad." She wasn't sure just how important he would think it was. At least he'd asked her about it. Usually, when Dad was reading, especially if it was a computer magazine, he didn't hear anything.

"When did you last have it, Darci? Try to think back," he suggested.

"It must be somewhere in your room, dear," Mom said.

Her parents were trying to help anyway.

Darci frowned. "Well, let's see." When did she write in it last? All at once, an idea hit her. Now she remembered. "Oh, yes," she burst out. "It was the day Donny got his new hamster, the day—" She broke off. She couldn't say it was the day Travis phoned, the day when she'd called him adorable in her diary. How could she forget that? "I know I had it in my room then. But I don't know why it isn't there now."

"Mom's good at finding things," Dad said. "Turn her loose on it."

Darci started quickly for the stairs. She wasn't too eager to turn anyone loose on her diary, not even Mom. "I'll go take another look," she told them.

As she passed the upstairs hall phone, she decided to call Luanne. Maybe Luanne would have an idea. With

30

Donny downstairs and Rick safely in his room with his door closed, no one could hear her talking on the phone.

She dialed the number.

"Luanne," she said after Luanne had answered the phone, "guess what?"

"He called again?" Luanne's voice rose with excitement.

"No." Darci couldn't even smile right now. "Remember my diary? I showed it to you one time." She'd never let Luanne read it, though.

"Sure, I remember. I'll bet you have a lot of good stuff in it by now." Luanne's voice sounded wistful.

"Well, I guess I do." She'd be embarrassed for even Luanne to read it. "But I can't find it. I've looked all over the place."

"Are you sure your brothers didn't rip it off? That sounds like brothers to me. I don't have any, but—"

"No, I don't think so. They don't seem to know anything. I asked them. Rick wouldn't pull a mean trick like that anyway. And Donny can't read a whole lot. He wouldn't know what it's all about. They don't act guilty, either one."

"So when did you have it last?"

"The day Donny got his hamster. I wrote in it that afternoon. It was right after Travis called." Her face felt warm just telling Luanne about it.

"Well!" Luanne was quiet for a moment. "So who else was in your house that day? Any of the other guys, like maybe Matt or—"

Matt! A terrible idea darted into Darci's brain, and it buzzed around and around in there. Matt! "Oh, Luanne! You don't think! Oh no!" She remembered the afternoon clearly. After Travis had called, she had rushed up to her

31

room to write all about it in her diary. All the boys had been in Donny's room. Later, she remembered she had seen Matt in the front hall before he went home. And he had smiled at her in kind of a funny way. "Luanne! When Matt left that day, he had a weird smile on his face."

"Guilty like?" Luanne asked, breathing into the phone with excitement. "Like someone who'd just ripped off a diary?"

"Oh, maybe. Oh, Luanne!" Darci groaned at a terrible new thought. "Maybe he's sitting over in his house right now, reading it." She remembered another part now she'd written after going to the movies one afternoon. It was about kissing and wondering what it would be like. "I might try it some day," she'd written. "I hope he won't have bad breath or gooey lips, whoever it is."

"Oh, Luanne! Do you think Matt would really do a rotten thing like that?" Even though Matt was a pest sometimes, she'd never thought he was that bad. Donny thought he was the greatest, and Rick liked him. Still, she felt hot and sick and sad at the idea of his reading all those things about her, especially that part about wanting to know Travis. What if he'd told the other guys. "Oh, no!" she exclaimed. "This can't be happening!"

"Hey, Darci. It's okay. Listen, maybe we're wrong anyhow." Luanne was trying to make her feel better. Darci tried to believe what Luanne was saying. But it was hard to forget such a terrible idea. And what could she do about it? Ask him? Oh, no. Tell him she had a secret diary? Then he'd tease her about that and might even start looking for it.

"It's probably there in your house somewhere, Darci. Bet you'll find it tomorrow."

So the next morning Darci got up early and searched all

around the house again. She went through the books on the shelves in the den, checked all the magazine piles in the living room, looked in the dining room, but it was nowhere. The last place she could think of was the trash.

She went out to the kitchen and found Mom breaking eggs into a bowl. Dad had just come in the back door and was standing there in his jogging clothes.

"When are you coming jogging with me again, Darci?" he asked.

"Oh, some other day, Dad. Right now I'm looking for that—uh—notebook again. Mom, do you think it could've been carried out to the trash, somehow?"

"Anything's possible, I guess," Mom said. "Why don't you go take a look?"

"Want me to come help you?" Dad offered.

"No, that's okay, Dad." Darci suddenly wondered what Dad would think of a notebook filled with scribblings about Travis. Dad probably thought it was for her school-work. If he knew it was all about boys and kissing—Darci felt her face getting red. "Thanks, anyway, Dad." She hurried out the back door and went behind the garage to the trash cans. She poked around through layers of news-papers, news magazines, Dad's and Rick's sports maga-zines.

Mom was always trying to throw things away. Dad was always trying to keep them. There were also egg cartons, milk cartons, cereal boxes, wrappings from Donny's bub-ble gum and Mom's panty hose. When Darci finally got down to some chunks of fat Mom had cut off a roast, some bones, and grapefruit rinds, she gave up.

Darci ran back into the house and headed for the kitchen sink to wash her smelly hands. "No luck," she reported. "All I got was a good look at the trash."

"Yuk! I bet it smelled," Donny said helpfully. He and Mom and Dad were sitting at the kitchen table together.

"It's just a shame." Mom shook her head. "I can't think where else to look." Darci knew that Mom was disappointed too. Mom had been pleased Darci had started writing in the diary—"letting it all hang out." Now Darci wished she'd let less of it "hang out." Mom probably wouldn't approve of all that stuff about Travis either. She had had a diary when she was a girl—red leather with a gold lock and key, she'd said. She hadn't said what she'd written about, though.

"What's so great about an old notebook?" Donny looked up from his cereal bowl. "Oh, I know. Maybe you had something in it about bo-o-oys," he crooned in an annoying way.

Darci felt really bugged by him. "Donny, quit it," she said crossly. She decided to ignore him.

"But, Mom, Dad, if it *is* in the trash, well, uh—" She had a sudden terrible picture of trashmen hovering around her diary, reading it—and laughing! "They just dump the trash somewhere, don't they?"

"Yes, in some remote canyon," Dad said. "So, you see, Darci, you can stop worrying." Behind his glasses, he gave her a little wink, as if he guessed what she'd written about. Did he? Did he know?

"You could get a new one," Mom added brightly. But it wasn't that easy to just figure it went out with the trash and forget it. Besides, if it was out in the trash, why hadn't Darci seen it? There hadn't been any trash pickup yet this week. And anyway, she never took her diary out of her room. She for sure didn't throw it in the wastebasket. So then where was it?

At school that day, Darci discussed it with her friends.

"It has to be Matt," Luanne said when Darci had finished. "Don't you guys think so?"

"It sure sounds like it," Jill agreed. "It couldn't just fly away. You better tell him to give it back."

They were tossing a Frisbee around outside on the playground together. It was a chilly day. The San Gabriel Mountains off in the distance were clear and blue. The playground was filled with mobs of kids who were running, screaming, and playing kickball. Just then they saw Susan coming toward them.

"Quick!" Luanne whispered. "Pretend you don't see her." Luanne slipped the Frisbee under her jacket.

They all moved into a huddle together. Jill fingered her braces. Lee busied herself with her jacket zipper.

Darci tried not to look in Susan's direction, but she did wonder what Susan was wearing today. She waited, expecting to hear Susan's voice calling out to them—that sure, loud voice of hers. But in a moment the footsteps had passed.

Luanne looked up and giggled. Darci glanced over her shoulder and saw Susan's retreating figure.

"Oh well," Luanne said, "she's probably looking for Debra." Debra and Susan were good friends.

Still, Darci wondered about that. "Do you think she wanted to hang around with us?"

Luanne shrugged. "She's not inviting us to her party. She doesn't need us. Maybe she's looking for Travis."

"Yeah." Jill frowned. "Don't you wish we could do something, like set off—uh, uh—stink bombs or something while she's having it?"

"Oh, Jill!" Lee laughed. "You just don't want her to have Travis there, that's all. Let's throw the Frisbee some more, okay?"

35

"We hardly know her," Darci pointed out as they broke apart and began to throw the Frisbee to one another.

"Don't want to either. She's too bossy." Jill reached up to catch the Frisbee.

"Well, listen, Darci," Luanne looked around to make sure no one else was listening. "What're you going to do about that Matt McGrath?"

"Maybe you could bribe him." Lee caught the Frisbee and threw a curve to Darci. Lee was good at sports. "You could make some of that good sour-cream dip, you know?"

"Want us to come over and help you talk to him?" Luanne suggested.

"Oh, that'd be great! Would you?" Darci held the Frisbee for a moment. She glanced over her shoulder but didn't see Susan anymore. "I've got to get it from that Matt." Maybe he hadn't had time to read it yet, at least maybe not the worst parts. He'd probably think they were the best parts. And if he told those parts to Travis!

At noontime, when Travis passed her in the hall, she could hardly say hi. She could barely look at him, much as she wanted to, and she knew her face turned hot pink. Adorable! What would he think of being called that?

That afternoon, Darci and Luanne and Jill and Lee waited out front in Darci's yard for Matt to come home. Pretty soon, he came down Rancho Street on his bike. When he saw the four of them just standing there, he skidded to a stop. "Hey, what's going on?" he asked. Darci thought maybe he did look a little worried.

"He's got it, I think," Luanne whispered. The four of them marched out into the street toward him. Now maybe he even looked a little scared.

"Don't tell him it's a secret diary," Darci said quickly. "I don't want him to know that!"

"What're we going to ask for then?" Luanne said.

"Just—you know—ask around," Darci answered.

They advanced on Matt. "What's up with you guys?" Matt swung off his bike. He eyed them uneasily.

"We just wanted to talk to you, Matt." Darci suddenly wished she hadn't started this.

"I think it's terrible to take things." Luanne tossed her blond ponytail.

"Especially some things," Jill added.

"What're you guys talking about?" Matt stared at them. "Take what?"

"We aren't really sure." Darci glanced at the others. "But Matt, if you do—uh, you know—have anything of mine, would you give it back, please?"

Matt's blue eyes, his whole face, looked puzzled. "Give what back? So you're looking for something, and you think I swiped it?"

"Well—uh—" Now Darci really wished they hadn't started this.

"It isn't fair to rip things off," Luanne said, positively.

"Look, you guys. I didn't rip off anything. I think you're all weird." Matt got on his bike and rode into his driveway. Then he stopped and looked back. "Better stay out of the sun. I'd say it must be getting to you. Yowee-e-e!" He let out a yell and vanished down the driveway.

Darci sighed. Now that hadn't helped at all—not at all. They went back across the street to her front yard and settled on her front step together. "Do you guys really think he has it?" Darci asked the others.

"It seemed as if he knew what we were talking about," Luanne said. "And besides, he had such a good chance to take it, being in your house and all."

"I think he did it," Jill agreed. She smoothed her dark hair thoughtfully. "Too bad you can't follow him right into his house. He's probably got it right in his room."

"Yikes! Think of that!" Luanne looked stunned. "If you could just go in there, check out his room—" She stood staring after Matt.

"Oh, sure. Break into his house or something," Darci scoffed. But how she wished she knew whether he had it or not.

The Letter

Darci kept looking for her diary but no luck. She searched her room once more, then went through the books in the den downstairs, under the furniture, everywhere she could think of. It was really mysterious. At breakfast, she asked Rick and Donny about it again.

"Haven't seen it, Darci," Rick said. "Sorry. Why don't you get Mom to give you another one?" Rick started to eat his breakfast.

She felt certain Rick didn't have it. He would never do such a mean thing.

"Donny, how about you? Are you sure?" She stared hard at him.

He slurped his cereal and looked up at her. "Why do you keep asking about an old notebook? Did you write something that's about a boy?" He trilled his voice in an annoying way. "Darci likes bo-o-oys."

"Donny, shut up!" She glowered at him. Still, she felt sure he didn't have it either. He probably couldn't read it yet, and besides, she could always tell when he was guilty.

So she just had to believe Matt had stolen it. And, oh, if he had, if he was telling the other kids about it, or showing it to them! The idea was too horrible to think about. If only she could get in his house—and in his bedroom! She'd have to get hold of him today and ask him again.

But she just couldn't talk about it on the way to school, not with everybody listening. And not with old blabbermouth Donny, who'd tell Matt what it was she'd lost. And Donny might start talking about how she liked boys again! She'd have to try to catch Matt later, maybe at lunchtime.

So after lunch, she and Luanne started out of the cafeteria to look for him. As they hurried down the hall, they saw Susan in the corridor calling to everyone to keep going. "Move on outside"—they could hear her important-sounding voice. "Come on! Move it!"

"She sure likes being the boss," Luanne grumbled.

"You're right," Darci agreed as they pushed open the double doors onto the playground.

"She ought to wear a T-shirt that says Bossy on it, instead of Luv Ya," Luanne giggled. Susan was wearing her Luv Ya T-shirt again.

But Darci was looking across the playground now for Matt. "Oh, rats! Too late," she exclaimed. Matt went racing by with a kickball in his hands, some other kids following him.

"What'll we do now?" Luanne squinted in the February sunshine.

"Hang around and wait for a chance, I guess," Darci said.

"He probably was just lying to us yesterday anyway," Luanne said. "Maybe he'll give it back today. When I think of all the stuff you must've written in it—"

Darci groaned. "Oh, don't talk about it. I'll just die if he's read it."

While they were standing there, they saw Jill and Lee come running toward them. "Look at this," Jill shouted, waving the school newspaper, the *Rio Reader,* at them. She stopped in front of them, puffing for breath. "Look!" She pointed at the paper.

"It says here that Susan is going to run things on Valentine's Day, and Debra is going to help her." Debra was the class president.

"Oh no! Those two get to do everything!" Luanne said.

"And guess what they're going to let us do—have valentines and cookies in our homerooms, as usual. Isn't that the pits! We've been doing that forever." Jill added, "While Susan is having a boy-girl party."

"You'd think when we got to be in sixth something different would happen," Luanne said.

"I wish we were in charge," Lee put in.

"I sure thought we'd get to do more things this year," Luanne grumbled. "Like hall monitors, for instance. The teachers just pick the same old kids all the time. In my cousin's school in Berkeley, they have kids who help in the cafeteria, kids who help choose the games they're going to play and the films they're going to watch. And my cousin's teacher even wears shorts to school too."

"Yow! Shorts!" Jill echoed. They looked at one another.

"I can't quite picture Mr. Polchek in shorts." Darci

laughed. "But it doesn't seem quite fair. We're getting older and they don't seem to realize it."

She reached for the *Rio Reader*. "Let's see what else is in here." She glanced through it. "Say, here's something in the Letters column. Some kid says he'd like to have better lunches."

"Who wouldn't?" Jill scoffed.

All at once, Darci thought of something. She looked up at the rest of them. "Listen! What do you think of this? Why don't we write a letter to the paper and say some of these things—how we're older now and how we oughta have more say and more chances to do stuff. And—and then why don't we suggest the whole class have one big Valentine party together."

"Terrific!" Luanne shook her blond ponytail excitedly. "Oh, Darci! Do you realize, if we had a school party maybe —maybe it would wreck Susan's? We could have it in the cafeteria. We could bring records and have decorations, and the cookies too, of course."

"Fantastic!" Jill agreed. "So who would care about Susan's old party at her house."

Darci looked at her friends. It was a super idea. "You know, it could work. Boys aren't that crazy about parties. I bet if they had one at school they might not want to go to another one that same afternoon. We could offer to bring the cookies, and we'll homebake them and make them really delicious. And the boys'll never go to Susan's!"

They all laughed. "Far out!" they agreed.

"You write the letter, Darci," Luanne said. "We'll all help you."

"Okay-y-y-y!" Darci smiled at her friends. "Let's figure it out right now. The best letter we can think of."

"Let's see—we could say we're more—more mature now in sixth."

"Yeah, and—and we have a lot of class spirit. Interest in our school and all that." Luanne grinned.

"Interest in Travis, you mean." Jill giggled.

They broke up laughing. Then the bell rang.

When Darci was back in her classroom, she took out her notepad and began to write.

We're in the sixth grade, and we're older now. Couldn't more of us take turns doing things at school—maybe be in charge more, like being hall monitors? Maybe have more to say, like about Valentine's Day. How about having a class Valentine party? Everyone could come to it. It would really make a lot of class spirit.

She had to shut her eyes for a moment as she thought about Travis—Travis at the party. He'd come, wouldn't he? *It could be in the cafeteria after school,* she wrote on. And then she added, *We would like to have more responsibilities.*

She sat back for a moment, feeling good about her letter. That was a great word to end it with. It sounded so mature! She wondered what Susan would think. Would she be waiting all alone in her house, maybe all decorated with balloons and paper hearts? And then maybe nobody would come?

Darci felt a twinge of guilt. But there'd be the school party. She could come to that!

"Class, let's quiet down now." There was the teacher, Mr. Polchek. "Get out your math books and let's get at it."

Darci looked hard at Mr. Polchek. Chubby Mr. Polchek —wouldn't he look funny in shorts! But Darci wasn't sure what that had to do with more responsibilities.

When Darci showed the letter to the others after school, they all loved it. They signed their names and then went together to drop it in the *Rio Reader* letterbox outside the principal's office. After they'd dropped it in, Darci felt a sudden worry. What if Mrs. Blair didn't like their letter? Or the teachers? Was it worse than complaining about the lunches? What if the other kids didn't like it? Maybe they'd even laugh! And what would Susan say?

But her friends seemed to think it was a great idea. They had to hurry off to get on their buses then, and Darci started for hers. If only they all rode on the same bus, but they lived too far apart. Then Darci saw Matt, alone at last. He was hurrying along the sidewalk toward the play-ground. She ran after him.

"Matt, wait. I—I want to ask you something."

Matt turned around. "Yeah?"

"Matt, if—if you did have anything of mine, would you just give it back? I—I could make you some sour-cream dip. . . ."

Matt kind of stared at her. "Man, you must really want it."

"So, do you have it?" she repeated. Oh, maybe he did. Maybe he'd give it back. "I—I'd really like it if you would—"

Now Matt was shaking his head. "Why is it such a big deal? I don't get it!"

How could he talk that way about her diary! "Well, it certainly is a big deal," she said crossly. "And if some people shouldn't have things that don't belong to them, then they . . . they oughta give them back."

Matt shrugged his shoulders. "Look, I tell you what. If I find it around—anything that looks like yours—I'll show it to you. If I don't see you this afternoon, I'll bring it to school tomorrow morning."

"To school? Oh no!" She dreaded the thought. Her stomach jumped. "Not to school! Why don't you just show me at home, okay?"

"Hey-y-y-y!" He shook his head. "So you don't want me to bring it to school, huh? This is weird." He glanced toward the playground. "Listen, I have to get to my game now."

He turned and ran off, and Darci watched him go, feeling sick. Now that hadn't helped at all!

Travis Comes Over

But Matt didn't show up with the diary the next day, or the next. And if he had it, he wasn't admitting it.

And now every time Darci saw Susan at school, she wondered what Susan would think about the letter in the *Rio Reader*. She found she didn't want to talk to Susan. She felt embarrassed. So she tried to avoid her.

Meantime, Travis kept smiling at Darci when he'd pass her in the halls. Was it a friendly smile or was he laughing at her? Did he know that she'd called him adorable in her diary? Oh, if only she knew whether Matt had it or not. She didn't know if she should smile back at Travis or pretend not to see him, but that was hard to do.

A few days later, he stopped her as she was walking on

the playground with Luanne and Jill and Lee. "Hi," he said. "How's that hamster?"

"Oh, uh, great," she managed to say. She felt Luanne's elbow poking her. She knew she should come up with something better than that. "Want to come over to see him?" How did she ever dare say such a thing? But now the elbow excitedly dug a hole in her ribs. She knew she'd said the right thing.

"Well, su-u-u-re." He leaned his arm against the wall of the school building and continued to smile. "What about this afternoon?"

"Oh, great." Darci felt the pressure of Luanne's elbow again. "Maybe we could all go to my house this afternoon, okay, guys?" she said, looking around at her friends.

Luanne nodded, beaming. "Sure. It's really fun over there."

"Well, hey now." Travis frowned. "That might be too many. Why don't you guys go some other day?"

He wanted to be with just her? Darci felt surprised and scared! As she stood looking at him, she felt that worry again. What if—what if he had heard about her diary?

"We don't mind." Jill shook back her dark hair as if she didn't really care. "We've got other things to do, haven't we?"

"Sure," Lee agreed loyally. "What are they?"

So she'd have to see him alone! But he wouldn't be acting this way, just normal like, if he knew about her diary, would he?

"Great then." Travis shoved off from the wall. "See ya this afternoon, Darci." As he walked off across the playground, Darci stared after him, feeling dazed. He wanted to come to see her alone?

"You really lucked out," Jill said in her ear.

"Yes, lucky you," Luanne said, her voice sad.

But Darci didn't feel so lucky. She felt worried. Besides, maybe he wasn't really coming to see her. "Maybe he's just coming to see Matt and Rick and the other guys on my street," she said.

"You could be right about that," Luanne agreed quickly. She looked more cheerful now. "Look, promise to call us the minute he leaves?"

Of course she would. She'd be dying to do that. But what would she do when he came? And how would she act? Expecially if he said he'd heard about her diary! Oh, then what would she do? She'd turn red and purple and pink!

When she got home that afternoon, she found Rick out in the kitchen.

"Where's Mom?" she asked. She wondered what Mom might say about Travis coming here. But Mom shouldn't mind her having a—a friend come over.

"Gone to psychology class." Rick went to the cupboard and set out a large jar of peanut butter.

"Well, uh, Rick, what do you like to do when you go see a girl?"

"Oh man!" Rick rolled his eyes and laughed. "What a question! Hey, I couldn't tell you. You're too young."

She felt a moment of worry. But of course Rick was just kidding. "No, really," she protested. "Tell me. Do you watch TV or listen to records, or what? Come on, Rick, I have to know."

Rick stopped smiling and reached for the peanut butter. "Ah, we listen to records and—uh—eat and— Say, what's a little girl like you want to know for, huh, kid?" he joked.

"Well, just in case anyone comes over to see me. Then I'd know what to do."

"Well, you can't beat eating." Rick knifed up a big

chunk of peanut butter and popped it in his mouth. Then he smiled at her.

Yes, she'd already guessed that. As soon as Rick left the kitchen, she began to fix a batch of garlic/green-onion sour-cream dip. She'd have that ready and a bag of potato chips. Her brothers always went for that. Then, let's see —how could she make sure her brothers and their friends didn't find it? She opened the refrigerator and tucked the bowl in the back of the vegetable crisper drawer. They'd never look in there!

Then she hurried upstairs to brush her hair. Her face looked pink. "Calm down," she said to herself. She frowned and fastened her barrette in her hair. If she sucked in her cheeks, would that make her look older? If only she had big blue eyes like Susan. She rolled her own brown eyes at herself in the mirror, but it reminded her of the dog down the street.

Was Travis really coming to see her? Did it have anything to do with her diary? "No, don't think about that," she told herself. Maybe he was just interested in hamsters. Uh-oh! She'd better go find the hamster.

She dashed out to the hall and into Donny's room. Good! There was the cage on the floor, and the hamster was sleeping, curled up in a corner in the wood chips. And good, too, that Donny wasn't around. She picked up the hamster cage and hurried downstairs with it. She set it on the front hall table. She and Travis could always talk about hamsters when he first came. She glanced out the window and was pleased to see Rick drive off in his car. Terrific! What a perfect time for Travis to come. Now if he only would.

She went into the den and placed a record on the stereo so all she had to do was press the button. But waiting like this was the worst. And the house was so quiet. She'd

49

phone Luanne, that's what. Darci started for the phone in the hall.

The doorbell rang. She stood, stricken. What if—if it was Travis! She felt terrified. And she wished suddenly that everybody were there, Rick and Donny and all her friends.

The bell rang again. Well, was she going to answer it or stand there in the hall like some kind of statue? Think! What would Susan do? She'd answer the door—for sure!

Darci hurried to the front door and opened it. There on the front step in the afternoon sunlight was Travis. He was wearing a camel-colored shirt with his jeans, and how cute he was! Those dark eyebrows and dark eyes. But she couldn't just hold the door and stare.

"Hi." She smiled and swung the door wide open. "Come on in."

Now he was coming through the door and into her hall —her own hall! It seemed almost unreal. "Talk," she told herself, "say something."

"Here's the hamster I was telling you about," she said. "I brought him downstairs. Donny usually keeps him up in his room." Maybe all he really did want was a quick look at the hamster and then he'd be off again. Might as well make it easy for him.

"Say, he's okay." Travis was peering through the cage. "What'd you say that African name was?"

"Bwana. Isn't that a crazy name? Do you want to hold him?" Darci started to open the cage door.

"No, let him sleep. Maybe later."

Later! So he was going to stay awhile. She wouldn't offer the garlic/green-onion dip yet, then. She'd hold that until she needed something more to do.

"Want to see my records?" She led him into the den. "I've got some good ones."

"Sure," he said. "What've you got?"

That was perfect. "I've got the Entertainers and the Bee Gees." Soon they were listening to music and talking about the records and various singing groups. Travis sang some of the words to a song called "Stompin'." Her heart beat so. She could hardly stop looking at him. And he said nothing—nothing at all about her diary. So she was beginning to feel pretty safe about that.

Tied Up

Suddenly Darci heard voices outside the house. Before she could say anything to Travis, the front door crashed open. There stood Donny and Matt in the front hall. Matt was carrying a big plastic bag. It looked like trash.

"I'm collecting cans for the drive for our volleyball team again," he said. He peered into the den at Travis and Darci, his blue eyes giving them a quick stare. "Donny says you might have some."

"Yeah, I been saving them for you, Matt," Donny said eagerly. "C'mon out to the kitchen. Say, whose bike is that out front, Darci?"

"It belongs to Travis." Darci tried to sound as if his bike could be there anytime. "We're listening to records." The music was very loud.

"I could've guessed," Matt said. "Where's Rick?"

"I don't know," Darci answered. "He just left." She wished Matt and Donny would leave also.

"Hey!" Donny frowned and pointed to his hamster in the front hall. "Who said you could bring Bwana down here?"

"I just wanted to show him to Travis, is that all right?" Darci wished Matt wouldn't stay there, watching them.

"I wanted to have a look at your hamster," Travis said. "I used to have one."

"Oh, okay." Donny started for the kitchen, and Matt followed him. At last! Darci got up to close the den door.

Travis smiled at her as she did it.

"Might as well keep the door closed," Darci explained.

Travis looked pleased. "Sure, sure. Good move."

"How about another album?" he said then, and got up to put a record on the stereo.

Darci sat down on the couch and, leaning back, thought how cute-looking he was. The music thudded in her ears. It was really loud. He came back and sat on the couch again too, a little closer to her this time. They sat listening and talking about the Bee Gees some more. Then, after a little bit, they seemed to have covered the field of music.

"Do you—uh—ever read the *Rio Reader*?" Darci asked, trying to think what to talk about now. What would he think of their letter to the paper? she wondered suddenly. "Did you ever write a letter to the paper?"

"Huh? Me? No, no. I don't write letters. Uh—do you?"

What'd she start this for? Next he'd be saying, "I suppose you write a diary too."

"Well, sometimes. My friends and I thought more kids would like to be in more things at school." Now she really wished she'd stayed out of this whole subject.

53

She jumped up. "Say, are you hungry?"

"What?" He looked a little surprised. "Hungry?" The music was pretty loud, and it was hard to hear.

"Yes. I've got some garlic/green-onion dip and chips." He must have quite an appetite by now. "Want some?"

"Well, sure, I guess."

She went over to the door and started to pull it open. But it seemed to be stuck. She grabbed the door knob and pulled it harder and harder. "What's the matter with this door?" She twisted the knob back and forth.

"Maybe it's locked," Travis said, coming over to her.

"But it doesn't have a lock."

"Here, let me try it." Travis seized the knob and turned and then pulled it with all his weight. Then, over the noise of the loud music she heard a sudden burst of laughter from the other side of the door.

Then Donny's voice shouted out "It must be lo-o-o-ve" in a dumb, silly way. Oh, how embarrassing!

"Donny!" Darci yelled through the door. "Open this door! Right away!" She shook the knob hard, the way she'd like to shake that Donny right now. But it didn't do any good. "Donny!" she shouted again, but he didn't answer. She turned back to Travis. "Look at that, will you? He's got us locked in here somehow."

"Say, too bad." But Travis was grinning. "Why do you think he did it anyway?"

"I don't know." She frowned. "He's just a big fat pest, that's what."

But Travis just laughed. "We might have to stay here awhile."

Oh, what was he thinking? If he had read her diary, maybe he'd think she wanted the door locked shut, wanted to be locked in with someone who was adorable.

Now she felt all red and hot and cross. "That Donny!" she exclaimed.

Then a new thought came to her. Maybe Matt was behind all this. "I'll bet I know who's in back of this. I'll bet it's that Matt McGrath."

"Yeah? You think so?" Now Travis looked amused.

"I'm going to get those two." Darci rushed over to the window. She raised it and threw her leg over the sill. A rush of cold air blew into the room. "I'll be back," she said, "just as soon as I catch them."

"Hey-y-y-y, wait a minute!" Travis headed for the window after her. "I'll come too."

"Well, if you want to." Darci straddled the windowsill and looked down at the ground below. It wasn't far. She slid over the sill and dropped to the yard below.

Travis jumped down after her. "I don't see anybody," he said, straightening up.

"Well, we will!" Darci marched grimly around the corner of the house to the front yard. There was nobody in sight all up and down the street.

"They're probably in the house," she said. She ran over to the front door and threw it open. "When I get hold of them—" she began, and then stopped. The front hall was empty but there was something new! There was a rope. The rope ran from the den doorknob to the foot of the stairs where it was tied to the bannister.

"Look at that!" she exclaimed, staring. "So that's how they did it!"

Travis was laughing. "Ha ha. Man, they really meant to keep us in there, didn't they?"

But Darci didn't find it funny at all. And the way he was looking at her with those laughing eyes! Oh, what did he think? And she could feel her face getting red. "Where are those guys?" She looked around the house crossly. "Where've they gone anyway?"

"Hey, I'll untie the door." Travis went over and began to pull at the rope.

Darci looked in the living room and the dining room. It could take the rest of the afternoon to find them. "Those —those big pains!" she exclaimed again.

Travis still had a little smile on his face as he pulled at the rope on the doorknob. And that made her feel so embarrassed. She went over to help him with the rope, and in a minute they had it off and the door open once more. So maybe now would be a good time for the food.

"C'mon out to the kitchen," she said. "We can have something to eat anyway. I made some dip for us."

"Great," Travis said. "I could go for some munching about now."

Darci headed for the kitchen with Travis following her. Now at least, this part should be okay.

"I left it in here," she said to Travis as she opened the refrigerator. She reached for the vegetable drawer. "That way no one—" She stopped talking. In the vegetable drawer, there were some carrots, some zucchini, but no bowl of dip. She cast a quick, anxious look around the kitchen. Uh-oh! There was the bowl over by the sink. "Oh no!" she exclaimed. She rushed across the kitchen and found herself staring at the bottom of the bowl, empty— but not quite. A few white streaks of dip remained. Automatically, she scooped up a bit and put it in her mouth. It would have been good—maybe the best she'd ever made. Travis reached in and licked his finger too.

"Guess we're too late, huh?"

"I'm sorry, Travis." Her eyes felt warm and moist. Those guys! They'd eaten all her dip. "Want a few—" She reached for the potato chip bag. A few crumbs spilled out.

"Well, I have to go," Travis said.

"Okay," she answered. What else was there to say? "Sorry about—things," she said, following him to the front door.

"Hey, that's okay." He strolled out the door. Darci followed him outside, and in a few minutes he was pedaling off down the street. Darci watched him go, feeling very sad. What a mess the whole afternoon had been. He'd probably have a way better time at Susan's house. He'd never want to come back here again. Just wait till she got hold of that Donny. And that Matt! Where were they anyhow? She'd tell them off for sure!

Getting Back
at Matt McGrath

After Travis left, Darci turned to go back inside when she suddenly heard laughter—boys' voices going "Ha ha ha ha" around the corner of the house. She went storming after them, and there in the bushes were Matt and Donny, laughing and laughing together, especially Matt.

"So it was you two!" Darci glared at them. "I just knew you two tied that door shut."

"But Darci, it was only a joke." Donny looked a little worried now.

"Well, it wasn't funny. Not at all! And Matt, I'll bet you thought up that whole idea. Donny could never tie a knot as good as that either."

"Hey, Darci." That annoying Matt was still snickering. "We just thought we'd have some fun, that's all."

"Well, I wish you'd go have fun at your house and leave me alone. And who ate up all my dip?"

"Oooops!" Matt cast a guilty glance toward Donny. "Guess we blew it, Donny."

Donny looked almost frightened now. "Uh—oh." He rolled his eyes toward Matt. "I thought Mom made it for us."

"Hey, sorry about that, Darci," Matt said. He almost looked it. "I didn't know that was yours."

"Well, I just wish you'd—you'd leave things alone. Tying the door shut like that!" And she went storming off again. What a terrible afternoon it had been.

At dinner that night, Mom said, "I hear you had a visitor this afternoon, Darci." The tone of Mom's voice meant she wanted to know more. Donny must have told her.

Darci's breath caught and for a moment she couldn't answer. If Mom and that psychology teacher were going to say she couldn't have Travis over—!

"It was just a friend, Mom. His name is Travis. He's new. He—uh—doesn't know many people." Actually, he seemed to know the right ones anyway, like Susan and her friend Debra.

"Well, that's nice." Mom smiled at her. "Boys and girls should be friends. They should just accept each other as people without a lot of fuss." Darci was so relieved she almost fell out of her chair. She stole a look at Dad and wondered what he thought about all this. But his eyes seemed to be smiling at her behind his glasses as he said, "Maybe it's okay to make a little fuss for certain friends."

"I'm sorry I wasn't here to meet him," Mom added. "Is he a nice boy?"

"Oh, yes, Mom, really."

"I'll bet he isn't as nice as Matt," Donny put in loudly.

"Oh, Donny," Darci protested. That Donny. What did he know? "By the way, why does Matt have to keep coming over here all the time anyway? You'd think he could find something else to do."

"He's my friend." Donny's mouth began to turn down.

"Oh, sure. He's way too old for you," Darci scoffed.

"Maybe he likes it over here," Dad put in. "I would if I were a kid."

"He has no siblings," Mom pointed out. "He probably gets lonesome." Mom and her psychology. Besides, Darci knew Matt had a lot of friends.

"But should he come here and scare away my friends?" Darci appealed to her parents. Maybe Travis hadn't been scared exactly, but he had left early.

"What's so bad about being tied up in the den for a while?" Rick took another slice of meat loaf off the platter. "Doesn't sound scary to me." He looked slightly amused, and Darci felt deserted by her own family.

But if her family wasn't very sympathetic, her friends were. When she described what Matt and Donny had done to her, Luanne said, "That was really rotten! You ought to get back at him, Darci."

"Terrible," the other two agreed. "What could you do to him?" It was Saturday and they were all sitting up in Darci's room.

"I just saw him out front with your brothers," Jill added. Darci went to the window and peered out. Yes, there he was, playing ball with the other boys.

"Of course, I suppose you could say being shut up in a room with Travis isn't all bad," Lee said thoughtfully. "I mean, some kids would like that. I bet Susan would."

"Well, he'll probably never come back." Darci dropped the curtain and groaned. "He'll probably have ten times more fun at her house at her party. Unless our letter to the *Rio Reader* helps us get a class party. Even then—"

"Oh, I hope it does. That'd be so super-r-r." Lee laughed.

"How was it anyway, having Travis here?" Luanne asked curiously. Darci hesitated. How could she admit to her friends how much she'd liked being with him and watching him sing, and how they'd sat on the couch, not that far apart either.

"It was fun," she said. "Except"—now she frowned— "I kept worrying about whether he'd heard about my diary." The thought of him knowing all her ideas about him, about kissing, and wanting to be more grown up, just made her squirm.

"Have you looked anymore for it, Darci?" Jill asked.

Darci nodded. "Sure. I've searched the whole house several times. I wish I could believe it went out with the trash. But I searched that too."

"Suppose Matt does have it," Lee said. "Do you really think he'd show it around? I mean—"

"Oh, don't." Darci covered her face. "I'll die if I think about it anymore."

The boys' shouts drifted up from their playing outside. Luanne got up and peered out the window. "Let's go out front," she suggested. "Maybe we'll think of something we can do to that Matt."

"Okay," Darci agreed. They all jumped up and pulled on their jackets and went hurrying down the stairs. If only they could do something, something that would find her diary.

But when they came out the front door, all the boys were just starting off down the street on their bikes—Rick, Matt, and Rick's friend William. Donny and his friend Jon were running along the sidewalk after them.

"Where do you think they're going?" Luanne said. She sounded disappointed.

Darci could see that Matt had one of those big plastic bags slung on his handlebars. "I think they're going to collect cans for the aluminum drive," Darci said. "Matt's collecting for his volleyball team."

"Matt does some good things sometimes," Jill said.

"But look what he's been doing lately," Luanne objected.

"I know." Darci sighed, looking after him. "Listening in on my phone calls, taking my diary—well, maybe—locking me up in the den—"

A car started to back down Matt McGrath's driveway, and Darci saw that it was Mrs. McGrath. She waved. "That's Matt's mother," she said to the others. "She's really nice. She always goes to the market on Saturday morning while Mr. McGrath plays racketball."

The car came backing slowly down the driveway into the street. But Luanne was looking over at Matt's house with a strange expression on her face.

"Darci!" She rushed over to her. "Why don't you just sneak into Matt's house after she goes?"

Darci stared at Luanne. Go in? Into Matt's house? While he wasn't there? "Luanne, I—I can't do that!"

"But she's leaving."

Mrs. McGrath called out, "Hello, girls."

Luanne shrugged. "Maybe she'd let you look anyway."

Darci watched the car. It was almost out to the street now, and Mrs. McGrath poked her head out the window. "I'm off to the market," she called. "You know how we all have to eat." She smiled.

"I've got an idea," Darci whispered to the others. "I'll just ask her now if I can go in."

"Good idea!" Luanne prodded Darci.

Darci ran across the street and over to the car. "Mrs. McGrath, I think Matt might have something of mine. Could I go in your house and take a look?"

"Why, of course, Darci. Just run right in. I left the door open for Matt." She glanced over her shoulder and started turning the car slowly in to the street. "What is it anyway? Maybe I've seen it."

"Uh, sort of a book," Darci said. She didn't dare tell Mrs. McGrath it was her secret diary, because Mrs. McGrath might tell Matt.

In a moment, Mrs. McGrath had driven off down the street, and everything was quiet again. Darci waved to her friends to come over. "She said we could go in," she called. The others came running across the street.

"So let's go." Luanne beamed. "That was great, Darci."

"I guess." Darci glanced toward Matt's house. She and Donny had been in and out of his house quite a bit, but not so much lately. Still, she had permission now. "I feel sort of funny about this"—she hesitated—"with Matt not here and all."

"I think it's okay," Jill said. "Besides, look at all the things he's done to you lately. And his mom said you could."

"I'll go if you guys do," Lee said. "But"—she glanced around uneasily—"let's hurry before Matt gets back here."

"Come on, then," Luanne urged.

"Well, okay." Darci still had this worried feeling about it. But it was a tempting idea. If they did find her diary— She smoothed her hair, then refastened her barrette in it. "Let's go," she said.

So, in a tight little group, they advanced across the

driveway and the front yard, the grass crunching under their feet.

"Let's just ring the bell anyway," Darci whispered. Somehow that made it seem more okay.

Of course, no one answered the door. They could hear the bell echoing and echoing within the house. In a moment, they pushed open the front door and stepped inside. It was a funny feeling, standing inside Matt's house with nobody there. They stood for a moment on the red-tiled floor of the front hall and looked all around. Matt's house was a Spanish stucco style too, like Darci's and so many others on Rancho Street.

"Where shall we look first?" Jill whispered.

"I guess Matt's room," Darci said. "It's upstairs."

"Let's hurry." Lee looked scared.

"Come on, then," Luanne urged.

They scurried up the stairs like mice. At the top was Matt's room. Of course, Darci had been there in the past with Donny or Rick. When they all reached his doorway, they hung there, staring inside.

"Quick! Let's search his room." Luanne was the first one inside it.

Darci stepped inside too and felt funny again. Should she be here? Now that she was, she had to look. She felt a shiver of excitement. Her diary—she'd get it at last, maybe. She glanced around his room, inspecting his bureau, his shelves, his books, his rock collection, a goldfish in a bowl, a lot of odds and ends, a corkboard with a lot of pictures and papers tacked up on it. But her diary— Where was it?

"Look!" Jill giggled. She was pointing toward two pictures of a very heavily muscled man and a caption below that read: "You too can look like this world-famous weight lifter." The weight lifter was flexing his arms, showing his muscles. And down on the floor were several weights that Matt evidently practiced with.

"Ha ha." Luanne, Lee, all of them clustered around, laughing. "Matt thinks he's going to look like that!"

"No way!" Luanne shook her ponytail.

"No, he never can," Darci agreed, but she felt like a spy. Maybe the others felt that way too, because now they all paused after they'd looked over his room.

And Lee said, "I use my brother's weights sometimes." But they couldn't talk about weights now.

"What'll we do?" Darci whispered.

"Well, uh." Luanne advanced toward the bureau, then halted.

"I don't see any small, brown notebook, Darci," Jill put in.

"I know." Darci frowned, disappointed.

"Should we search his room some more?" Luanne's voice wavered.

"Oh, I don't know," Darci said. "You mean open the drawers and all that?"

A car could be heard coming down the street, and they looked at one another. But the car passed, and it was very quiet again.

"I think we better get out of here," Darci said. The thought of searching Matt's room, poking through his desk and bureau drawers chilled her. The whole feeling of being here seemed sort of awful.

"I agree," Lee said quickly. "I mean, let's split."

"Okay, okay," the others said, and they all turned and started out of the room. But just as they reached the head of the stairs, they heard a door slam downstairs, toward the back of the house.

They froze like four statues.

"Someone's here!" Luanne hissed.

Then they heard footsteps down below.

"I didn't hear any car, so it must be Matt," Jill whispered. "Where can we hide? We don't want Matt to find us in here, do we? That would be so embarrassing!"

"Follow me," Darci said. She turned and darted across the hall to the bathroom. The others rushed in after her. Darci eased the door almost shut. "Sh-h-h-h," she whispered. She didn't exactly want to meet Matt now either. It would be too awful!

They stood huddled together, listening, in the small yellow room. They could hear Matt moving around downstairs.

"I have to go," Lee whispered with a longing glance at the toilet.

"You can't!" Jill said flatly. "Hold it!"

They stood, listening again. Below, they could hear more footsteps, getting loud, coming toward the front of the house.

"Oh, no," Luanne moaned. "What if he comes upstairs —what if he has to—" Now she threw a desperate glance toward the toilet.

But he was coming! They could hear footsteps on the stairs, pounding and pounding—up toward them—

"Get in the shower!" Darci ordered. She pulled open the door of the stall shower. They squeezed in, and Darci pulled the door shut after them. But couldn't he see through the shower door? If he came in the bathroom and happened to look this way, wouldn't he see four bodies in there? Oh, what would he think? That they were all taking a shower with their clothes on? But where else could they hide?

Darci looked around at the others' frightened faces. They could hear noises now from Matt's room, thumps and bangs. Luanne rolled her eyes toward the ceiling and began to sway. Darci shook her arm. "Luanne," she whispered, "cool it!"

But now they heard him again—footsteps out in the hall, going down the stairs at last. Luanne exhaled loudly and opened her eyes.

"Luck-y-y-y!" Jill whispered. They all stood there, limp and listening. There came the slam of a door.

"I think he's gone," Darci said. She eased open the shower door and darted to the bathroom window. Below, she could see the driveway, and suddenly, as she watched, she saw Matt go whisking by on his bike, another plastic bag on his handlebars.

"He's gone," she said aloud.

"Let's get out of here." Jill and the others all pushed out of the shower.

"You're sure, Darci?" Luanne said.

Darci nodded. "I saw him go down the drive. "C'mon, let's get moving."

They pulled open the door of the bathroom and ran down the stairs. By the front door, they paused.

"Let's check," Darci said. She opened the front door a crack—no one to be seen. She opened it a little wider—still an empty street—

"Go!" Luanne urged. "I wanna get out of this house."

In a minute they were out, hurrying across Matt's yard and across the street, and that was when they heard a noise down at the end of Rancho Street. It was Matt McGrath rounding the corner, coming back up this way, the other guys behind him.

"Look!" Lee's voice shook. "I mean, we got out just in time. Here he comes!"

They froze, looking at Matt as he came toward them. He had a big bag of cans stuffed inside the other bag on his handlebars. It must've ripped or something, and he'd come back for another one. The other guys stopped at William's house, but Matt didn't. He headed for the girls, angling his bike over toward them.

"What're you guys doing anyway? Just waiting for me?"

Darci could hardly think what to say. If he knew what they'd been doing— She could feel herself getting hot all over.

"Oh, we were just looking around," Luanne said quickly.

"But we're through now," Darci added. They started up Darci's walk while Matt stared after them curiously. Darci didn't even like to look at him. If those blue eyes of his could see into her brain, he would know just what she'd been doing!

Garlic/Green-Onion Dip

"What's the matter, Donny?" Darci asked the next morning at breakfast. Donny seemed to be sad. He kept stirring his cereal around but not eating it.

"My hamster's lost. When I woke up this morning, he was gone."

"Gone?" Darci echoed. "Not in his cage?"

"Uh-uh." Donny nodded and drooped over his cereal bowl.

"Maybe you didn't shut the door tight," Rick suggested. "Maybe he's still in your room."

"Let's go look for him now." Darci started to get up.

"I already did." Donny's voice was mournful. "Me and Mom looked and looked."

"You should say 'Mom and I,' Donny," Mom corrected. She set a bowl of bananas on the table. "Better eat now. I'll be vacuuming in there right after breakfast, so I'll keep searching for him again."

"Poor Bwana. He was so neat." Donny's mouth turned down.

"Well, those are the breaks, kid." Rick reached for the cereal and a couple of slices of toast.

"I'll help you look again after school." Darci bit into her toast and felt sorry for her brother. Poor Donny. It was too bad.

As Darci and Donny started up the street after breakfast to catch the bus, Matt McGrath came out of his house. Darci looked nervously at him. Did he have any idea they'd been in his room Saturday? Maybe his mom hadn't told him anything.

"Did you hear Donny's bad news?" she said quickly, and she was relieved when Donny began to tell him about losing Bwana. But as Donny talked, Darci realized something else. Now she couldn't invite Travis over to see the hamster anymore.

"I'll help you hunt for him," Matt was saying. "One time I lost one, and I found him under the refrigerator."

"Ya did? Maybe that's where mine is." Donny was smiling now.

That was nice of Matt. As she listened to him talking to Donny and cheering him up, she wondered if he really did have her diary. After all, they hadn't seen it in his room, and he'd never said anything yet that made it sound as if he'd read it. But she didn't want to start thinking about poking around in his room again. It gave her that guilty feeling, in spite of the things he'd done to her. Travis hadn't come over again since the day that Matt and Donny tied the den door shut. But at least Travis was still speaking to her, although she'd noticed he talked to Susan, too, sometimes. Darci got a tight, sad feeling when she thought about Travis going to Susan's party. Well, maybe there would be a class Valentine party. If only their letter in the *Rio Reader* would do some good, if it ever came out.

That afternoon, Darci helped Donny search for his hamster. There was a note from Mom, saying she'd gone to her class and that she'd looked for Bwana while cleaning Donny's room. They tried to look under and behind the refrigerator, but it was hard to see. Then they went upstairs and hunted all around up there except in Donny's room, since Mom had already done that.

Donny scowled. Darci could tell he was disappointed. "Let's try downstairs again," she said.

"Okay," he agreed, and followed her back down the stairs.

"Where's Matt?" she asked as they bent to peer under the dining-room table. "I thought he was coming over to help you." Not that she wanted him to. She was just wondering.

"He had volleyball practice," Donny answered. They finished searching in the dining room, checked around in the den, and had just started in the living room when the doorbell rang.

"Say, maybe that's Matt," Donny shouted and dashed to the front door. But in a minute, Darci heard him calling, "Darci, it's for you."

Darci crawled out from behind the green, stuffed living-room chair on her hands and knees and looked up toward the front door. Oh no! There was Travis, standing in the doorway, smiling at her. "Oh, hi!" she said. Why did he have to find her like this? She jumped up quickly and pushed back her hair. It must be all in a mess. But how adorable Travis looked. He was wearing a bright red shirt and jeans. "Come on in," she managed to say.

"Just thought I'd stop by. You playing some kind of game?"

What a cute smile he had and what a little kid she must look like down on the floor. But at least she had a good reason. She laughed, embarrassed. "No, you see my brother's hamster got lost. We've been looking all over the house for him."

"Say, too bad. I'll help you."

"Oh, neat!" Donny exclaimed.

"We just had this last room to do," Darci said quickly.

So the three of them went all over the living room together, and Darci kept stealing little looks at Travis. She could hardly believe that here was Travis, that cute Travis, crawling around her living room. But he was probably getting bored. He might want to leave soon.

"Well, guess we can't find him, Donny." Darci stood up. "Travis, are you hungry? Want me to make some of that dip like the batch I made the other day?"

"Su-u-u-re!" Travis smiled. "That sample I had was the greatest!"

Travis followed her out to the kitchen where she nervously started to put together another batch of garlic/green-onion dip in the same green bowl. If only it would turn out to be as good as the other.

"Want me to help?" Travis scattered the powder in the sour cream while she stirred it. How wonderful he was!

"Let's hope there are some potato chips," she added, reaching into the cupboard. There were! A fresh, crispy bag! So maybe everything was going to be all right this time. At least Matt wasn't here to wreck things. She wished she could ask Travis something about Susan's party.

"Do you like parties?" That was as close as she dared get to the subject.

"Sure, sometimes." He smiled at her. What did she expect him to say? That he wished she could come to Susan's party too?

"Depends on who's there." The way he smiled at her then! Her heart began to bump around inside her chest.

"Let's go into the den," she said, leading him out of the kitchen.

"Say, you really know how to treat a guy, Darci," he said following her. "Good chow, good music, a place to ourselves." He settled down on the couch in the den and began to eat. "Great," he said, munching away. "Really fantastic, Darci."

Darci looked at adorable Travis chewing her dip and chips and couldn't believe how lucky she was. "Glad you like it." She smiled at him. "Want to listen to some Bee Gee records again?"

"You know it!" He grinned. "We were kind of interrupted last time, weren't we?"

She wasn't quite sure what he meant, but she guessed he meant they'd only been partway through the records.

"Right." She smiled back at him. She got up to put a record called "Far-out Night" on the stereo, and after it started she went back to the couch. But Travis had moved to the middle, so she had to sit close to him. Was this what Mom would call being friends? Darci was glad Mom wasn't home right now anyway.

Travis rocked his body to the music and mouthed some of the words. This filled her with admiration for him, and she swayed her head a little in time to the music too.

Suddenly, he moved closer to her. "Hey, Darci." Now he had his arm around her shoulders. She felt a little worried. Rick didn't tell her about this part. Now he was pulling her toward him, and as she stared dumbly into his face, she smelled wave after wave of garlic/green-onion dip. It was so strong it almost smothered her. It was one thing to eat it—delicious! But to smell it after someone else had eaten it, while it was still churning around in someone else's stomach—yuk! And she must smell the same way! She had to look away for a moment and get a breath of fresh air.

Just then, there was a crash of the front door, and she heard Donny shouting out in the hall, "Matt, Matt, come on in the house."

"Oh, no," Darci groaned.

Travis eased back and frowned a little. "Trouble again?"

"I hope not," Darci said fervently.

Travis reached for the remains of the dip, and Darci almost wished he wouldn't. If he was going to kiss her, she wished it could be less smelly. She'd never really been kissed before, not a real kiss the way they do in the movies. If only she had thought about all this before she made the dip. Rick had never said what kind of food to have.

But now the record was ending, so she'd better get up to change it. This time, when she turned back around again, Travis was right there behind her and smiling down at her, and moving closer and closer.

But just then, the den door burst open, and there was Donny with Matt behind him. "Darci! Matt says we've gotta look in here for the hamster. Come on in, Matt. It's okay. See, I told you. They're not doing anything."

Darci could feel herself getting red in the face. What did that Donny mean anyway, about not doing anything!

"But, Donny," Darci protested.

They came marching into the room, and Donny added, "Matt brought his flashlight so we can really see."

"But, why in here?" Darci frowned. "You've got the whole rest of the house to hunt in."

"Because. Matt says there're a lot of dark places in here that we missed." They dropped to their hands and knees and began shining the flashlight under the couch and the big chair. Matt kept smiling in a funny way.

"Hi, Travis," he said.

"Uh, hi." Travis didn't sound very enthusiastic.

"But still, you don't have to look in here," Darci protested.

"Yes, we do," Donny insisted. "Hamsters like the dark."

"There're all those books, you see." Matt nodded toward the bookcase. "We'll have to look behind all of them."

"Yeah," Donny breathed happily. "You're really neat to help me, Matt."

"Su-u-u-re," Matt said with a quick look at Darci. "I'm neat."

"Well, guess we better get into the act." Travis rolled his eyes and shrugged toward Darci. He started for the shelves. "I'll look in this row."

Darci just watched for a moment. She felt as though somehow or other the situation was getting out of control. "With this whole house to look in," she repeated, "it seems funny—" But what could she do? Maybe try to get rid of them as fast as possible. She dropped to her knees and started to look behind the books too. As she slid them off the shelves, she thought, this is just like being little kids. Travis, the cutest boy in the whole sixth grade comes to see me, and we're hunting for a lost hamster with my little brother and Matt McGrath. A hamster that's maybe even dead by now!

And after a while, Travis said he had to go, and he went

out the front door and climbed on his bike and rode off.

Things just didn't seem to go right whenever he came over. He'd probably never come again. He'd probably prefer some of those more mature types, someone like that Susan, for instance.

In the News

The moment Darci leaped off the school bus on Wednesday, someone shoved a copy of the *Rio Reader* at her.

"Here, you better read this," whoever it was said, and ran off. Darci stood there with the crowd from the bus surging past her as she stared down at the school newspaper. Already her heart was beginning to jump around. Was the letter in?

A couple of boys pushed against her, but she didn't even look up. She was almost afraid now—that the letter would be in—or that it wouldn't. She opened the paper.

There was the Letters-to-the-Editor column. And—she gasped. There it was! She began to read. Oh, yikes! It was just as they had written it. Nobody changed it or fixed it up or anything. She read to the end. It was signed by Darci, Luanne, Jill, and Lee. Their letter, all right! Oh, wow-ee!

"Darci!" She looked up. There were her friends, running up to her. They had copies of the *Rio Reader* in their hands too. They all gathered in a huddle and read it and re-read it.

"Oh, isn't it terrific!"

"It's far out! Fantastic!"

Darci smiled around at all her friends. "We did it, didn't we? The only thing is—" Now she stopped smiling. "What'll we say when we see Susan?"

Luanne shrugged. "We can pretend we didn't even know about her party."

"Right," Jill agreed. "I even sit right next to her, and she didn't say anything to me."

"I hope I don't meet her anywhere," Lee said nervously.

"Well, besides, nothing's happened yet!" Luanne pointed out.

"That's right," Darci agreed. "And maybe nothing will. The food didn't get any better in the cafeteria just because someone wrote a letter about it."

That morning there seemed to be copies of the *Rio Reader* everywhere, and everyone seemed to be reading it. What did the other students think? Darci couldn't tell exactly.

At lunchtime, Mr. Polchek said to her, "You wrote that letter, Darci?"

"Yes," she said.

"Well." He rubbed his chin. "Well, well."

But what did that mean? Did he like it or not? Maybe not. Maybe teachers wanted to go on picking the same monitors. Maybe they didn't like the idea of a class Valentine party. Was it a good letter or not? It was hard to tell what Mr. Polchek was thinking.

"Did Miss Stein say anything to you about it?" Darci asked Jill and Lee while they sat eating lunch.

"Sure." Jill shrugged. "She said it was good to practice writing. She said everyone should write more letters, to our grandmothers and everybody. And they should keep a diary too." Jill made a face. "She said it would be good to let out our feelings and all that."

"She should know what happened to you," Lee said to Darci.

"You're right," Darci sighed. She just wished she hadn't let out so many feelings in her diary, or hadn't had the feelings in the first place. But how could you help your feelings?

"That doesn't tell us what she thought of our ideas though," Luanne objected. "I still think a class party would be a lot, uh, fairer." Luanne smiled knowingly at all of them.

"To us anyway." Jill giggled.

That afternoon during Darci's math class, Debra, the friend of Susan's brought in a note from the principal. After Mr. Polchek had read the note, he looked up.

"Darci, Luanne," he said, "Mrs. Blair would like to see you two girls in her office after school."

Darci's heart thumped with sudden fear. Why, oh why? There was a sudden buzz from the class, and Matt turned around and looked back at Darci and rolled his eyes.

"Quiet down, kids," Mr. Polchek said. "Mrs. Blair just wants to talk to the girls about their letter, that's all."

All? Darci caught the glance Luanne sent her. How could he say "that's all"? Luanne looked worried.

"By the way, class," Mr. Polchek was going on, "writing letters is very good practice." Darci groaned inwardly. These teachers—all they thought about was teaching. What did he think of their ideas? And what would Mrs. Blair say? That was the biggest worry now.

But during the afternoon recess, several kids came up to Darci and Luanne and said they liked the letter and wouldn't it be neat to have a class Valentine party!

But how about Susan? She probably hated the idea. Now, how could they face her? What would it do to her party?

Darci whispered this to Luanne as they were going down the hall after school. And there was Susan up ahead, calling to some kids to keep going.

"Well"—Luanne shrugged—"so she doesn't like it. We didn't like her idea either."

They stopped in front of Mrs. Blair's office. Lee and Jill would be coming along in a minute, and it was almost time to see Mrs. Blair.

Just then, Travis came hurrying up to them. "Hey, the letter writers!" He grinned.

Oh, he was so cute! Darci could hardly breathe. Those dark eyes! "Hi." Darci smiled. If only he would ask about Donny's hamster, say something about coming over again.

"We've been looking everywhere for Donny's hamster," she said.

"Hey, good, good." He leaned against the wall, his hands in his pockets. "Sure hope you find him. Your brother was really down, wasn't he? Say—that was a great letter. And so you'd like a class Valentine party, huh?" How amused he sounded.

"Well, sure." Luanne wagged her ponytail. "Why not? Then everyone could come."

"Yeah, yeah." He lifted his eyebrows at Darci as if he were impressed. "Everybody. I get your point."

But now Susan was coming down the hall. "Hi," she said. "Look, I have to tell you to go on outside. You can't hang out in the halls. Hi, Travis." She smiled at him. Today, Susan was wearing a short pink sweater, and her gold earrings sparkled in her ears.

"We're waiting to see Mrs. Blair," Darci explained, just as Jill and Lee came along and joined the group.

What did Susan think of their letter? She had said hi to them at least.

"It's my job to tell you to go out, you see." Then she looked at Travis as if she wanted to say, "But not you, Travis," and she shook back her hair so that her earrings shone.

Just then, Mrs. Blair's secretary came to the office door and called to them, "Girls, come in now."

As they started into the office, Darci's legs suddenly felt like rubber. Oh, what now? Was Mrs. Blair mad? Darci wasn't sure which was worse—trying to deal with Susan or Mrs. Blair. The secretary led them through the outer office into Mrs. Blair's office.

"Come in, girls," Mrs. Blair said. She looked small as she sat behind her desk. But her dark eyes always seemed to see everything, know everything. Darci felt hot, nervous, as she and Luanne and Jill and Lee moved into the room, bumping into each other.

"Sit down, won't you?" Mrs. Blair waved toward some chairs. Luanne stumbled and almost fell into hers. Darci knew Luanne was scared because she felt that way herself. What did Mrs. Blair think of girls who criticized their school?

But after Darci and the others sat down, Mrs. Blair leaned back, and for the first time, smiled at them. She had slightly tanned skin with faint, fine wrinkles, like the figs Mom sometimes bought. Fig skin. Hadn't she even written that one time in her diary? Fig-face! Oh, how terrible it would be if that diary should turn up at school. Darci thought for a moment she would freak out, absolutely freak out right now! She tried to get rid of those thoughts in case Mrs. Blair could see right straight into her mind.

"I want to talk to you about your letter in the *Rio Reader*," Mrs. Blair said. Darci felt her stomach tighten up. Mrs. Blair might say, "Don't you realize there's a party that day already? Or are you trying to ruin it?"

But Mrs. Blair said, "It's good to see you girls taking an interest in your school and wanting to help make things better."

Darci sagged against her chairback with relief. Mrs. Blair wasn't mad! "We—uh—like our school a lot," Darci said, glancing at her friends. That Berkeley school they'd been discussing one day didn't really sound better, did it?

Again Mrs. Blair smiled, like a sun on a cloudy day.

"Well, I've talked with the teachers. We've decided to open up the system more, let those who want to sign up for hall monitor duty, if their grades are okay. We have some other plans too." Darci held her breath. What about the Valentine party? "And discussions are under way about a class Valentine party. Would you girls be willing to help?"

"Oh, yes, yes, of course we would," they all said quickly.

"Then, fine. Darci, you'll be in charge of decorations, and you others can be on the committee."

And so it was like a dream. And they weren't in trouble, and everything good was going to come true.

But as they rose to go, Mrs. Blair said, dryly, "So you girls wanted a party for everyone?"

"Oh, yes," Darci said quickly. "Everyone." Travis too, her mind insisted upon thinking.

Afterward, when Darci told her parents about it, Mom looked pleased. "Why, you girls have managed to do just what we were trying to accomplish at our PTA meetings —more student participation, more sensitivity to the needs of the students—" Mom broke off, smiling at her.

"Way to go, Darci," her dad said. "That shows real leadership."

Darci didn't know it meant all those things, but if her parents thought so, well, great!

That night, Darci wished she had her diary. She would really like to write in it now and tell all this good news. And if she could, she would say, "So we're having a class Valentine party. What will happen to Susan's? Will hers be better? And I'm in charge of decorations. If only everybody will come to ours! Like Travis, I hope!"

Just When Things
Look Good

The next morning, it was gray and raining outside. Maybe it was the gray skies that made Darci feel so worried. As she looked out her window, up and down Rancho Street, she wondered if her diary was out there somewhere. If so, it would be ruined by the rain.

But maybe she felt worried because she was thinking about Susan and dreading meeting her at school. Susan would probably be furious. It was a new feeling, making someone hate you. And yet—and yet—look what Susan had planned to do, have her own little party, with Travis!

At school that morning, everyone was talking about the class Valentine party and everyone seemed to love the idea.

"Fantastic!" the other kids said, and they kept coming

up to Darci and telling her they were really glad she wrote that letter to the *Rio Reader*.

"Thanks, Darci," a girl named Jessica said to her. "It was so great of you to do this for the class." Darci felt a little guilty thinking about it. Maybe she'd been thinking of being with Travis most of all. How was Susan going to take it?

Then that very day, Darci was assigned to her first turn at being hall monitor. So soon! At lunchtime, she hurried to the office to get the monitor's badge she would have to wear.

"Try to keep the halls quiet, Darci," Mrs. Blair said, "so the other classes can get their work done." While the fourth, fifth, and sixth grades went to lunch, the three lower grades had classes.

Darci's hands felt cold. "Yes, Mrs. Blair," she said.

"It won't be easy. Everyone will have to stay inside today. That's why we need lots of monitors."

The weather had turned nasty—a late return of the rainy season, with rain falling hard all day. All the kids would have to play in the gym. Usually it was sort of fun, with everyone racing around in the gym, yelling and laughing. But Darci wouldn't be doing that today.

"You stand by the cafeteria door, Darci. As they come out, urge them quickly toward the gym. No stopping and talking. The other monitors will do the same."

"Yes, Mrs. Blair." Darci rubbed her hands together nervously. Well, she'd just tell them, that's all.

Darci hurried to her post by the cafeteria door. Right away, a big bunch of boys came out and started to push each other around in the hall.

"Go to the gym and do that," she told them.

They didn't seem to hear her.

"Go to the gym, you guys," she said more loudly.

"We like it here." One of them grinned.

So okay, she was used to guys. She could handle this. "Go to the gym right now"—she raised her voice—"or I'll take down your names and report you." She pulled a pad out of her pocket and glared at them.

"Okay, okay." They went rushing off down the hall.

She could see the next monitor—it was Debra—standing at the gym door, waving them on inside.

Darci let out a breath. She just had to get tough, that's all. Some more kids came out and laughed loudly. "Don't be so noisy." She went over to them. "The other kids are in classes, you know."

"We weren't doing much," she heard one grumble to another.

"Yes, you were," Darci felt like saying. Then she had to call out to some others, "On to the gym."

Just then, Travis and Brian came out the door.

"Hi." Darci smiled at Travis.

"Look who's monitor." Travis stopped and smiled at her. "How're you doing? Anybody giving you a hard time?"

"No, not much." Darci swung her arms as if it were no trouble at all.

"Hey, Larry!" A kid in a plaid shirt bellowed, bursting out of the cafeteria. A bunch of fifth-graders followed him.

"Quiet!" Darci ordered.

"Yeah? Who said?" the kid said. Now all the kids bunched around him. He threw something in the air. A red Frisbee. The crowd surged toward the Frisbee, yelling.

"Would you guys be quiet!" Darci tried to glare at them. "Cool it and get on out of here."

"Yeah?" They sneered at her.

"Yeah." She put her hands on her hips. "Get going!" She didn't care if she sounded bossy.

"Yeah"—all the boys mimicked her—"get going!"

What could she do? Those bratty kids! She moved toward them threateningly, but they just laughed. "I'll take down your names." But what were their names?

"Hey, you guys," Travis spoke up. "You heard her. Now beat it or—" He stepped forward.

"Yeah, bug off," Brian added.

Now the fifth-grade boys looked impressed and began to move down the hall. "Okay, okay," they muttered.

Darci took a deep breath. This wasn't so easy, being a monitor. She turned to Travis and Brian. "Well, thanks. That was a big help," she said gratefully.

"Sure, Darci. See you later." Travis smiled at her. That Travis was so neat and so nice to help her.

She would've loved to talk to him some more, but along came a bunch of giggling girls. "Quiet!" She frowned at them.

It was busy like that the whole time. Darci was really glad when her time was up and the bell rang.

"Hi," she called when she saw her friends coming up the hall.

"Darci! How'd you like it?" They looked at her monitor's badge. And she felt important again.

"Okay, okay," she said, trying to sound cool.

"Good," Luanne said. "I hope I'll be able to do it all right when my turn comes. Oh, Darci, everyone's talking about the party, and—"

"Hi!" There was Susan, in front of them. "I just heard the news. So you guys put it through, I hear." She was wearing her green jade earrings again.

"You mean the class party?" Darci looked at her and felt the worry again.

"Say, I've had the greatest idea! I offered to have the whole class over at my house for the Valentine party. And Mrs. Blair just now said it would be okay. Don't you think that's really far-out? Won't that be so much better than the smelly old cafeteria?"

Darci glanced at the others. "But I thought you were having your own party."

"No, I'm giving that up so I can have the whole class over."

"Are you serious?" Luanne asked. Luanne looked like a kid whose balloon had just burst.

"Of course. You should see our playroom. We've added a whole gigantic room to our house."

"You sure it's big enough for everybody?" Luanne didn't sound pleased. No wonder! It would be Susan running things again.

"No problem!" Susan looked self-confident. "You should see all the games we've got: pinball, Space Invaders—" Susan rolled her eyes. "Ping-Pong, of course, a big stereo, and we have wallpaper that looks like mirrors."

It did sound great, a thousand times better than the cafeteria. "What about decorating it?" Darci asked. The picture of herself running a committee to decorate the cafeteria was fading far, far away.

"Oh, all you guys on the committee are supposed to come over early that day and put up decorations. We'll have a bunch of streamers and hearts and balloons and stuff." Susan peered down the hall. "Listen, there's Debra. I have to go." She raced off down the hall.

Darci and Luanne and Jill and Lee walked on down the hall in silence for a moment. Then Luanne said, "I wish one of us were having the party instead."

"I know," Darci agreed. "But"—she let out a groan—"we don't even have a playroom."

"Who'd have one like that anyway?" Luanne sighed as they turned in to their classrooms.

"See you later," Darci said to her friends. She went to her desk and sat down, but all she could think about was Susan's fantastic playroom. One good thing, anyway, was that it was a class party and maybe Travis would come. It was a great spot for a party, and everyone would have a super time. Yet, the whole party idea didn't seem nearly so good anymore. Funny how Susan hadn't seemed to mind the change in plans.

Valentine Surprises

On Valentine's Day, something wonderful happened. When Darci opened her desk after lunch, there, next to the pile of valentines she'd received that morning, was a red heart-shaped box!

"What's that?" she said aloud. "Who put this in my desk?" She lifted it out and opened it. Inside was a small chocolate heart. How delicious it smelled, and it was all smooth and yummy-looking.

"Luanne," she called out. A few other kids were already back at their desks too. Darci jumped up and rushed over to Luanne. "Look! See what I found in my desk!"

"Darci!" Luanne bent over the box. "Is it—is it real?"

"Oh, you lucked out!" Some other kids crowded around too. "Chocolate!"

"Who gave it to you?" Debra asked.

Darci looked up at all the faces. "Why—I—I don't know." But she was already guessing. Luanne leaned forward and whispered, "Do you think it's from—?"

Darci pulled back and stared at Luanne, and then they both started laughing. Travis! Oh, it had to be from Travis.

"Looks good enough to eat," Matt said, pushing up to the crowd around Darci.

"Yeah, yeah, let's eat it," some of the other kids said.

"No way," Luanne said quickly. "It's too small to share with all you guys."

"Besides, I don't want to eat it. Not yet, anyway." Darci held it lovingly. "Isn't that about the nicest chocolate heart you ever saw?"

"Class!" Mr. Polchek called out. "In your seats now."

Darci went back to her desk, feeling all warm and happy. Getting this chocolate heart was like having a wonderful secret. Travis—Travis must like her! How she hoped he would guess who'd given him that gorgeous valentine that she and her friends had sent him. Jill had said at lunch that Travis looked really surprised when he'd opened such a big one, and everyone kidded him about it. And now it was going to be so much more fun to go to the Valentine party, even though it was at Susan's house.

After school, Darci kept looking for Travis, but she didn't see him. Well, she would at the party.

Darci persuaded Rick to drive her over to Susan's after school. On the way, they picked up Luanne and Jill and Lee at their houses. All of them were pretty excited. Jill kept combing her fingers through her dark hair and saying, "Oh, it's going to be so terrific!" And Luanne kept tying and untying a ribbon in the back of her hair. And Lee kept smiling.

"So you're going to have a far-out party, huh?" Rick said to them.

Darci sat up front with him. She had a scared feeling in her stomach. What if the party wasn't good? What if nobody came? "I hope so," she muttered.

Susan lived on Hillside Place, a hilly street where the houses were set farther apart. Susan's house was a low, modern type, white with red camellia bushes in bloom across the front, just right for Valentine's Day. There was a red paper heart on the front door.

"Thanks, Rick." They all jumped out of the car and hurried up to the door. But Darci couldn't stop that tight feeling in her stomach. They rang a chiming doorbell, and Susan answered the door. She was wearing a red dress, and she had on red heart-shaped earrings.

"See my new earrings," she said, happily pushing back her blond hair.

"Oh, nice. Really great," they all said, but somehow Darci didn't feel very happy about Susan's new earrings.

"Come on back to the playroom now." Susan led them through a wide front hall, past a large step-down living room. It looked like a terrific house.

They went through the kitchen, where there was a big punch bowl and paper cups set on the table, and out toward the back of the house.

"Here it is," Susan said, opening a door.

"It's great," Jill exclaimed.

"Fantastic," Lee agreed. "I mean, it really is." They were standing in the middle of a giant-sized game room. They gazed around. Sliding glass doors led out to a big green yard. On the opposite wall was the wallpaper that looked like mirrors, and there were games and a Ping-Pong table and a snack bar with stools where you could sit for eating and drinking.

"It's wonderful," Darci said. "Really, Susan. You have a perfect place for a party."

"Glad you like it." Susan smiled. "I worked on it all last summer. Thanks for offering to help." She pointed to the Ping-Pong table, which had a pile of crepe paper and red hearts on it. "Here are some thumbtacks for the streamers. And here"—Susan went over to the Ping-Pong table—"is a big net. Maybe you can put some balloons in the net, then tie it up on the ceiling. See those hooks up there? That's where we usually tie it. Then later we can undo the net, and all the balloons will come floating down. We do that for New Year's Eve parties."

Darci kept looking at Susan. Susan didn't seem at all cross or unfriendly. It was really amazing. Maybe she didn't mind having the whole class come over.

Susan left after that, and Darci and her friends looked at one another. So Susan had told them what to do after all. But somehow it seemed okay. The net and the balloons did sound like a good idea.

"Well, let's get going." There wasn't a whole lot of time. Darci pushed up her sleeves. She'd worn her best new green pants and green sweater. But could that compare with heart-shaped valentine earrings? She hoped she looked good.

By the time they had the crepe paper streamers and red paper hearts hung all over the room, the place looked just great! Now they could hear footsteps and voices coming through the house.

"Hi." There were Travis and Brian. "Oh, man!" The boys gazed around the room, impressed.

"Fan-tastic!" Travis turned to Darci. Oh, those dark eyes! He really was adorable.

"You like it?" Darci smiled back. She wanted to rush over to him and say thanks, oh, thanks, for the chocolate heart. But now she knew he liked her for sure, so she kept on smiling at him. "We're just about to blow up the balloons." She explained the whole idea about the net and the balloons drifting down later.

"This is going to take forever," Luanne groaned, puffing into a balloon, "and it's almost time for the party."

"Want me to go ask Susan for a bike pump?" Travis offered.

"Oh, good idea." Darci was relieved. There were so many balloons, and it would take so much air. "Thanks, Travis." She gave him another big smile.

"Maybe you could tie them up in the net for us too," Jill added. "Doing all this work makes me thirsty. Don't you think we could go get one little drink of punch?"

"Sure, go ahead," Travis agreed. "We'll tie up the net for you. Won't we, Brian?"

"Sure, sure." Brian smiled.

That Travis. He was so nice. Darci hurried toward the kitchen with Lee and Luanne and Jill. It was almost time for the party to start, and everything did look so great. She didn't feel worried anymore.

Out in the kitchen, Darci was surprised to find Miss Stein making punch and Susan hurrying around helping her. For the first time, Darci realized she had not seen Susan's mother.

By now all the kids were arriving, crowding down the hall and through the kitchen and out to the playroom. The house seemed crammed with kids. The music boomed from the stereo speakers. The games clicked and whizzed and whammed and beeped. Kids were dancing, laughing, yelling. And so many were telling Darci, "Hey, thanks for the great idea. This party is far-out."

"You really did a good thing, Darci," someone else added, "when you wrote that letter to the *Rio Reader*."

Darci looked around the room and felt proud. "It does seem to be turning out okay, doesn't it? It was great of Susan to have us, wasn't it?" She had to admit that.

"Yeah, Darci!" There was Matt with a couple of other guys. Matt! Even he had come! "The games are the greatest," he said. "This was some good idea."

"Yes, Darci, you've done a very good job with the decorations." That was Mr. Polchek! Her teacher was complimenting her! "Those balloons will be a nice touch when they come floating down," he added.

So everything was good. Darci noticed that Susan was busy hurrying back and forth to the kitchen, bringing in dishes and paper cups and things. She wondered again where Susan's mother was. Maybe she worked, the same as Lee's mom.

Then Darci wandered over to a table where there were some snacks. She ate some of the chips and dip. It was delicious. It wouldn't be as smelly as the kind she made.

"Who made this, do you know?" she asked Susan who was just hurrying by. "It's really good."

Susan paused, her arms full of paper cups. "I did, Darci." The red heart-shaped earrings swung in her ears. "It's easy to make, just mix up cream cheese, sour cream, and canned clams."

Susan went rushing off again. Darci was thinking she should follow her and offer to help, when Travis appeared.

"Darci, you wanna dance?"

"Oh, sure, Travis." She beamed at him, thinking about the chocolate heart. "I got some great valentines," Darci said as they pushed through the crowd toward the dance area.

"Yeah?" He grinned at her. "I did too. Thanks," he added.

Oh, he knew, he knew which one was theirs! "Thanks to you too. Yours looks—looks good enough to eat." She smiled at him, feeling very clever.

He raised his eyebrows. He seemed surprised. "Yeah?" But they were so near the loud music now, it was impossible to talk.

They began to dance. Darci was glad she knew so much about dancing, because Rick had showed her a lot. Kids made room for them as they whirled and swung around. Travis was good, he really knew how to dance, and she loved to move to the music. Then when the music turned slow, he put his arms around her and pulled her close. To be this near to Travis, so near— She could stare right into his neck. Oh, what an adorable neck he had!

So things were turning out to be perfect. Mr. Polchek and Miss Stein were standing together, smiling and looking pleased. Now Susan and Debra were coming from the kitchen with the boxes of cookies the kids had all donated. Then Miss Stein carried in the large punch bowl and set it on the table. Someone lowered the music, and all the kids began to crowd around the food table.

"Let's go eat," Travis said. "I heard they've got some chocolate chip cookies."

"Yes, let's." Darci hurried toward the table too. And it suddenly occurred to her, maybe now would be a good time to let the balloons come floating down. She looked around for Susan to ask her if it would be okay. But Susan and some others were busy opening the boxes of cookies. Darci caught a glimpse of thick brownies and heart-shaped red iced cookies. They looked so good.

Darci turned to ask Travis if he would help her untie the net, but he was already over by the table and just reaching for cookies. Well, it would be a perfect time to have the balloons come drifting down over the crowd. Darci grabbed a chair, pushed it over near the hook in the ceiling, and climbed up on the chair. She stretched up as high as she could. Her fingers didn't quite touch the net where it was tied. "Ah-h-h-h," she groaned as she stretched harder. Her fingers pulled, loosening the net.

This time it came undone, and now the balloons would drift slowly down, the red ones and the yellow ones, the green ones and the blue—but wait! Something was going wrong, very wrong! Instead of drifting, some of the balloons were hurtling, smashing downward. Oh, why, oh—why were they crashing down so fast? And oh—smash! One plopped into the punch bowl, and red punch splashed out in all directions. And another—oh no! Why was Mr. Polchek rubbing his head—and water was running down his face and—oh! He was all wet!

"Mr. Polchek!" Darci screamed. "Mr. Polchek!" Oh what was the matter here? Darci went rushing over to him. Mr. Polchek was pulling at his shirt, loosening his tie, wiping his face with his sleeves.

"Mr. Polchek, what happened? I don't understand." She stared up at her teacher, aghast and amazed.

Mr. Polchek looked down at her. "I don't either, Darci. Ooof!" he grunted, pulling his collar away from his wet neck. "I thought you were in charge of decorations."

"Oh, I was, I was. But—" But what? She wasn't the one who'd filled and hung the balloons. Travis? Darci looked at everyone crowded around Mr. Polchek. She saw the faces of her friends, of Travis and Brian. They all knew who had filled the balloons, but who was going to tell? Travis would, of course.

"I really don't understand this, Darci," Mr. Polchek was saying. "I thought you were in favor of giving the students more responsibilities and—"

Oh, she was, she was! But something had gone wrong!

"I'm really surprised too"—now Miss Stein was speaking—"that you, Darci, of all people— I suppose you thought it would be a joke to drop water balloons on the other students."

Why didn't Travis say something? Darci glanced toward him, but he'd eased behind someone, and she couldn't see his face. And Brian? Where was he? She didn't see him either. And her friends didn't want to rat on them and she didn't either. Who wanted to be that kind of a rotten person? But why weren't they speaking up, those guys? Everyone began to talk and whisper, and some had already gone back to the games.

"It's a terrible mess over here," Miss Stein called out. She looked very upset.

"Maybe I can help." Darci pushed through the crowd to the refreshments. The valentine paper tablecloth was soaked. A lot of the cookies were soggy and crumbling apart. The others were being grabbed up by the kids and eaten. "Miss Stein, I'm sorry. I don't understand. I don't know—"

"I don't think there's much you can do about it now," Miss Stein said stiffly.

"I'll go get some sponges." Darci headed for the kitchen. She felt like crying—like freaking out. What a mess! This was the absolute worst! She looked around for Travis but didn't even see him.

But there was Luanne. "Oh, Darci, how did it happen?" And now all her friends were there around her, patting her and trying to mop up the table.

"Darci, aren't you going to tell?" Luanne whispered.

Darci frowned. "I—I don't want to rat on them."

Jill shook her head crossly. "But it's not fair!"

"It isn't," Lee agreed.

Darci realized that Susan was right behind her. And to her surprise, Susan said, "Poor Darci." Then, her arms full of trash, she went hurrying off. Before Darci could think anymore about Susan, she looked up and saw Mr. Polchek coming.

"Darci," Mr. Polchek said, drying his face with a paper towel, "I'd like to see you about this later."

"Y-y-yes, Mr. Polchek." What else could she say, or do? She put a bunch of the soaked cookies and paper plates in the boxes and started for the kitchen.

"We'll clean up the rest here," Luanne called out to her.

The music was playing, and Darci walked past the kids who were playing games, yelling, and laughing again. Why did this happen? Why did Travis do that? She looked around, and there he was beside her.

"Darci," he said, his face flushed. "Listen, me and Brian, we never thought it would turn out like this. We only meant to water bomb a couple of kids. And—and we really want to thank you for not ratting on us. No kidding, that was great of you, Darci, and your friends too."

He—he wasn't going to tell at all? She stared at him.

"Ya see, we're on the volleyball team, and Polchek's in charge. He'd—he'd be really tough on us, ya know?"

No, she didn't know. Didn't he understand that it was hard on her too? She opened her mouth. "I think—"

Darci saw Susan rushing by again, carrying more cookie boxes filled with trash. She must go help Susan.

She started for the doorway, then looked back at Travis. "I thought you were so great—to give me that chocolate heart and all."

"What chocolate heart?" he said.

What chocolate heart? Did he really say that? Darci walked out to the kitchen in a daze. Was he kidding? What was going on today anyway? People weren't acting the way they were supposed to at all. Take Susan— She'd said, "Poor Darci."

In the kitchen, Darci dumped the boxes in the trash cans. She could still hear the music and laughing, but she didn't want to go back to it anymore. She'd call Rick for a ride, go home instead. But the line was busy when she tried from the kitchen phone. So maybe she'd get her jacket and start walking. She'd tell Susan later how sorry she was.

She was just going out the back door when a voice called, "Darci, wait!"

It was Susan. This time Susan really would be cross, like sizzling mad probably. She must think Darci was trying to ruin her party.

"Darci." Susan hurried over to her. "That's not fair what Travis is doing. You're being pretty nice not to rat on him."

Darci could only stare. Susan knew? But of course! Susan had given him the bike pump for the balloons.

"Look, Darci, I—I really think it's shabby of him." She laid her hand on Darci's shoulder. "And thanks a lot for helping so much today."

"You—you didn't mind having the whole class?"

"No, I liked the idea." Susan smiled. "I've been wanting to get to know everybody. I loved it."

"Oh." Darci couldn't think for a minute. "And your— your mom, will it be okay with her?" Darci looked around the messy kitchen and wondered why Susan's mother wasn't home yet.

"I don't have any mother. I live with my dad," Susan said quietly. "He thought having the class party here was a great idea. It's sort of a mess now though, isn't it?"

No mother? Susan would have to do all this work?

"I should stay and help you clean up, then." Darci reluctantly let go of the door.

"No, no, you don't have to. Debra has a clean-up committee. You already helped enough. 'Course you can stay though."

"No." Darci turned toward the door again. She didn't want to. She just wanted to get away. "I—I have to go now, if it's okay with you. Bye, Susan." And she went on out the back door and left the house and the noise of the party behind her. This whole day was turning out to be one big shocker!

"You'll Be a Hero"

Darci walked for several blocks down Hillside Place. She felt almost numb from all that had happened with Travis and the balloons, and from all that she'd learned about Susan. Susan didn't have a mother. Susan had done the whole party herself. Darci couldn't get over the shock of this. But what about Travis?

Suddenly, Darci heard a whistle behind her. Was it Travis? He'd come after her? He'd confessed who really filled the balloons with water, and now he wanted her to come back to the party?

She whirled around, beaming, ready to call out to him. But when she peered up the street behind her, what she saw was Matt McGrath coming toward her on his bicycle.

"Hi," he said, pulling up to a stop. "I decided you must've left the party."

"Yes," she answered, surprised he'd noticed.

"And so you're all alone?" Did he think Travis, or no, maybe her friends were with her? He glanced around at the empty street and sidewalk. "Yeah. I guess you are alone."

It was late afternoon now, and the sky was turning gray.

"I am by myself," she answered. "I thought I'd walk home now, after all that mess at the party."

"Oh, yeah," he said, but he didn't go on. She stared down at the sidewalk for a moment. Of course, he'd seen the whole terrible thing that had happened.

"Say," he said abruptly, "do you want a ride home on my bike?"

She glanced up in surprise. His blue eyes looked so friendly. "It's pretty far, you know," he added.

"Sure," she said. "Thanks, Matt." She went over to him and sat on the crossbar of his bike. He pushed off from the curb and started to pedal down Hillside Place. She nervously tried to tuck her hair inside her jacket collar so it wouldn't blow in his face.

"That's a bummer about the balloons and all that," he said.

She looked down at his hands as he steered the bike. There were a few freckles on the backs of them, friendly freckles like the ones on his nose.

"It was terrible," she said. "Unreal!" She had to hold her lips tight and squeeze her eyes shut for a moment so she wouldn't cry.

"Ye-a-a-ah," he said. Then he was quiet. And the only sounds were the squeaking of his pedaling and the whish of the tires on the pavement.

"And they thought you did it?" he said.

She shrugged, glad she could talk to him over her shoulder and didn't have to face him. "I was in charge." Her lips trembled again. "So they blamed me."

"Oh, man!" he exclaimed. He was quiet again, and the bike creaked under them as he pumped up a slight hill. "You wouldn't do that. No way."

She shook her head, unable to speak for a minute. Besides, now they were turning onto Robles Avenue, and cars and a truck rumbled noisily past.

"So who else was helping you?"

"My friends Luanne and Jill and Lee."

"And? Anybody else?"

She nodded. Did she have to keep this secret from Matt too?

"Well, who did it then? Why didn't they admit it instead of laying all this on you?"

Darci's hair blew across her face. She brushed it back out of her eyes and a few tears too. She couldn't talk. Her whole face felt quivery and sad. And she remembered how Mr. Polchek had said, "I thought you wanted more responsibilities, Darci." Oh, how that had hurt, taking that quote right straight from her letter in the *Rio Reader*. It was hard—hard to be in charge and try new things. It would've been safer to keep doing it the old way, having valentines and cookies in their homerooms, like little kids. Now all this trouble seemed so unreal!

"And so you didn't tell?" Matt persisted.

She shook her head. "No, I didn't." Of course, she'd thought Travis would do his own telling. True, he probably would get in a lot of trouble with Mr. Polchek and might be put off the team or something like that. But now what was going to happen to her? At least Susan had figured it out and didn't blame her. That was the one good thing about it. Susan, who had no mom. Matt steered the bike around a curve. Up ahead was Rancho Street. "You know something? Maybe I can guess who did it," he said. "Yeah," he added after a minute. "It all adds up. I bet I know."

He was figuring it out that Travis had helped her. Travis and Brian, because he knew they were always hanging around together. She wondered what Matt would have done. Would he have let her take the blame?

"So are you pretty mad at them?" he said.

She waited while a bus and a string of cars streamed past them. Then she shrugged her shoulders again. She wasn't exactly angry, just, well, sad—that was it—and let down somehow. Someone she'd thought was so great, well, now he didn't seem so great after all. And the choco-late heart! She'd thought he'd given her that too. So that was another weird thing. If he didn't, then who did? Some other boy in her class? Maybe Steve, who sat next to her and borrowed her eraser all the time. Or—or—oh, it couldn't be Matt, could it?

"Look, Darci," Matt said. They bumped over the drive-way at her house, and the bike squealed to a stop. "I'm sorry you had such a rotten time."

"That's okay, Matt." She slid off the bike and faced him. She tried to shrug as if it all didn't matter. "Things hap-pen like that, I guess. Thanks for the lift."

"Besides, some of the kids will know you didn't do it, and they'll think you're really terrific for not ratting on the guys who did. See, you'll be a hero."

"A hero? Oh, sure!" She could almost smile at that. "Well, thanks again, Matt." She started for the house. Nice of Matt to try to cheer her up though. But she wasn't exactly a hero to Mr. Polchek or Miss Stein. Although Susan had been rather admiring, and nice too. She thought about Susan in her terrific but empty house. How would it be, being on your own like that? No wonder Susan was so bossy. She was used to being in charge, had to be in fact.

Darci headed across her yard and up the front steps. It wouldn't be that much fun to come home every day to a house where there was no mom, even one who wouldn't let you have parties. She opened the front door. She heard Mom's voice talking on the phone. It was a good sound. If only she had her diary now, she could write down all these things. She'd let it all hang out. Mom's teacher would probably like that. And then at the end Darci would write, "But maybe Travis will call tonight, say he's sorry, say he's confessed to Mr. Polchek, say he's coming over."

A New Kind of Dip

But Travis didn't call all Friday evening. Only Darci's friends telephoned and said they just couldn't understand what was the matter with that guy. Was he some kind of a fink? And her parents said it really wasn't fair for her to have to take the blame.

Saturday morning there was no news from Travis either. Darci felt very sad. She talked to Luanne again. They discussed Susan too and agreed it must be hard not to have a mom. Luanne said Susan had been very nice about all the mess yesterday and did a good job of seeing that it was all cleaned up. But why, Luanne repeated, didn't Travis confess?

Darci had just hung up when she heard the boys' voices

in the downstairs front hall. Then she heard Donny calling out, "Look everybody, I've got a new pet."

The boys came clumping up the stairs, Rick and his friend William from down the street, followed by Donny. "Come on in my room and I'll let you see him," Donny said. She wondered what Donny had now.

And there behind them was Matt coming up the stairs too.

"Darci," he said in a low voice, approaching her. "I've got news."

"What news?" She stared at him.

"Listen," he said, "I want to tell you something. Brian just called me up."

"Brian?" She stared at him in wonder.

"Right. And guess what? Polchek found out. He figured it out somehow. Brian and Travis are going to get detention. But you're out of the soup, Darci."

"Out of the soup?" she echoed.

"Yeah, you're cleared. And Brian said they both thought you were great for not ratting on them, even if it didn't work out."

"Oh, Matt! Terrific! Oh, fantastic!" Darci beamed. "I'm really not to blame anymore. Are you sure about that?"

"Yeah, yeah." Matt nodded.

She was so happy, so happy. Out of trouble. Oh, wonderful! "Thanks, Matt. Thanks for telling me the good news. And that isn't so bad for the guys, is it? To get detention?"

Before Matt could answer, Donny yelled from his room, "Darci-i-i, come look at what I've got."

But Darci couldn't move, couldn't stop smiling. She was so glad, so relieved!

"Wanna go see what Donny's up to?" Matt asked her.

"Oh, okay." She followed Matt into Donny's room, and there was Donny, all red-faced and excited, waving around a cardboard carton in his hand. The others crowded close, as he opened the carton triumphantly.

"See?" Inside was a small brownish turtle. "And I'm gonna call him Bwana too."

"Oh, man!" All the boys laughed.

"Son of Bwana." Matt grinned.

"That one won't get away," William added.

"What a name for a turtle." Darci had to laugh too. Oh, she felt so good now. She felt like laughing at anything.

"Where are you going to keep him?" She glanced around at the messy room. The bedspread was half-yanked off the bed and—

Her glance caught on something, and she stared and stared. "What's that?" She darted forward. "My books! Donny!" She dropped to the floor. "Donny! You've got your bed propped up on my books." Several of her good horse books! They must've been missing from her room all this time.

"Well, you've already read them, haven't you?" Donny said. "You've got a whole bunch."

"But I want them. And it's not good for them." Darci ran her hands over the backs of her books. "You should prop your bed up with something else."

"How about these big wooden blocks?" Matt suggested.

"Yeah, that's fair, Donny," Rick put in. "C'mon, you guys, let's lift up the bed."

"Well, okay." Donny scowled.

Rick and William lifted the bed, and Donny shoved out the books. They scattered, and one fell open. And there lay a small, brown notebook.

"My diary!" Darci started for it. "I've been looking and looking for that." But Donny grabbed it first.

"Hey, who wants to read Darci's diary?" He waved it in the air.

"Donny!" Darci leaped toward him, but William snatched it away.

William opened it and began to read. "Tonight Luanne and I are—"

Darci grabbed for it. "William, give me that diary!"

William held it higher. "Let's see what's in this red-hot diary."

"Give it to me!" Darci rushed at him, but William handed it to Matt. Darci felt frantic. If they didn't stop passing her diary around and opening it and reading it— and now Matt had it!

"Here, Darci." Matt didn't even open it. He just handed it to her.

"Matt!" She seized her diary. "Why, Matt, thank you very much." She stared at him in amazement. "Thanks, Matt. That's really nice of you."

"Aw, Darci," William protested. "We weren't really going to read it, were we, you guys?"

"I was," Donny said. "Soon as I learn how."

Darci clutched her diary, her precious diary, at last, and glared at her brother. "Donny, how'd this get under your bed?"

"I don't know, Darci." Donny shrugged, and he rolled his brown eyes at her as if he were all innocence itself.

"Did you come in my room and get it?" Had he had the nerve to come in her room and dig into her bureau drawers? She felt furious with him.

But Donny just looked surprised. "I never saw it. Honest. I just grabbed up those books. They were there in your room, all in a pile. On your table maybe."

"Oh." She started thinking back. "So that's it." She must have left her diary there, in with her horse books on her bedside table that day—that day when Travis phoned. How amazing. She'd been in such a hurry to call her friends, she must not have put it away. Now she had to go tell Mom and call Luanne and the others.

"So, I guess all that's settled," Rick said. "Let's go, you guys." He and the others turned to leave.

She followed them out into the hall. The boys were thumping back down the stairs now, except for Matt, who lingered behind. He was looking at her.

"Darci, I do have something of yours." He reached in his pocket and held out his hand to her.

She bent forward to look at it. "My hair clip!" she exclaimed. She reached up to her hair. She had several clips and hadn't realized one was missing.

"I found it in my room," Matt said.

"Your room?" She stared into his blue eyes. That day they'd searched his room!

"Matt, I'm sorry." The things she'd thought about him! How unfair she'd been. How easy it was to make a mistake, to suspect someone unfairly. She looked at Matt's friendly face, his blond hair, and the way it fell across his forehead. He was being so nice to her. Then she had an idea.

"Matt, did you—I mean, uh, someone gave me a chocolate heart."

Matt poked her arm. "Did you like it? They were having a big sale at the market."

"Matt! Did you give me that?"

"Yeah, well, kind of a joke, ya know?" He looked embarrassed. "Got any left?"

"Oh, sure! You want some?" She smiled at him. "And listen, how about I make you a new kind of dip I just found out about." The clam dip she'd had at Susan's. It wouldn't smell as bad as the garlic/green onion. "And I'll bring it in the den, and we can listen to records."

"Great!" He grinned. They clattered down the stairs together. She'd bring down her favorite records, and afterward, why, she'd have to write all about this in her diary for sure.

About the Author

Martha Tolles is the author of *Katie's Baby-sitting Job* (available as an Apple Paperback) as well as two other books about Katie. She says, "My previous books have brought me many letters. One reader wrote to me, 'I wish you'd write about a girl who learns to get along with a brat of a boy on her street.' And so that's why I wrote *Darci's Diary*."

Her books are also inspired by her family, which includes five sons and one daughter. A graduate of Smith College, Mrs. Tolles lives with her husband in San Marino, California.

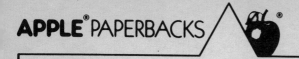

APPLE® PAPERBACKS

Delicious Reading!

NEW APPLE® TITLES $2.50 each

☐ FM 40382-6 **Oh Honestly, Angela!** Nancy K. Robinson

☐ FM 40305-2 **Veronica the Show-Off** Nancy K. Robinson

☐ FM 33662-2 **DeDe Takes Charge!** Johanna Hurwitz

☐ FM 40180-7 **Sixth Grade Can Really Kill You** Barthe DeClements

☐ FM 40874-7 **Stage Fright** Ann M. Martin

☐ FM 40513-6 **Witch Lady Mystery** Carol Beach York

☐ FM 40452-0 **Ghosts Who Went to School** Judith Spearing

☐ FM 33946-X **Swimmer** Harriet May Savitz

☐ FM 40406-7 **Underdog** Marilyn Sachs

BEST-SELLING APPLE® TITLES

☐ FM 40725-2 **Nothing's Fair in Fifth Grade** Barthe DeClements

☐ FM 40466-0 **The Cybil War** Betsy Byars

☐ FM 40529-2 **Amy and Laura** Marilyn Sachs

☐ FM 40950-6 **The Girl with the Silver Eyes** Willo Davis Roberts

☐ FM 40755-4 **Ghosts Beneath Our Feet** Betty Ren Wright

☐ FM 40605-1 **Help! I'm a Prisoner in the Library** Eth Clifford

☐ FM 40724-4 **Katie's Baby-sitting Job** Martha Tolles

☐ FM 40607-8 **Secrets in the Attic** Carol Beach York

☐ FM 40534-9 **This Can't Be Happening at Macdonald Hall!**
                   Gordon Korman

☐ FM 40687-6 **Just Tell Me When We're Dead!** Eth Clifford